THE CALL
OF THE WILD

AND

WHITE FANG

The Classic Library for Children

THE CALL
OF THE WILD

—•—

AND

—•—

WHITE FANG

BY JACK LONDON

CONDENSED AND ADAPTED BY
KATHRYN R. KNIGHT
CLAY STAFFORD

ILLUSTRATED BY
MICHEAL FISHER
JERRY DILLINGHAM

COVER ILLUSTRATED BY DOM D'ANDREA
PLATE COLORIZATION BY JERRY DILLINGHAM

Dalmatian Press

The Dalmatian Press Classic Library for Children
has been adapted and illustrated with care and thought,
to introduce you to a world of famous authors, characters, ideas,
and stories that have been loved for generations.

Editor — Kathryn Knight
Creative Director — Gina Rhodes
And the entire classics project team of Dalmatian Press

The *Call of the Wild* is the story of a dog
whose life is changed forever. Kidnapped
from his sunny California home, Buck is taken
to the cold, hard world of the Klondike.

Buck is hitched into the traces
of a dog sled, but the traces cannot hold
his spirit, his will, or his true nature—
to be wild—to be free.

Up in the frozen north, life is harsh and
dangerous. But this is where White Fang,
the wolf-dog, feels at home—in the wild.

When White Fang lives among man-animals,
he must learn to fend for himself.

And when he finds himself with a man who
is kind to him, he must learn to love.

THE CALL OF THE WILD

CONTENTS

CONTENTS

CHARACTERS

BUCK: a large St. Bernard/Scotch shepherd dog stolen from Judge Miller's estate in California

JUDGE MILLER: Buck's first owner

MANUEL: Judge Miller's hired gardener's helper who kidnaps and sells Buck

THE MAN IN THE RED SWEATER: the dog-trader who "breaks" Buck

PERRAULT AND FRANÇOIS: French Canadian dog-sledders who work for the Canadian Government, Buck's first owners in the Klondike

DOG TEAM OF PERRAULT AND FRANÇOIS:

CURLY: a Newfoundland dog bought at the same time as Buck

SPITZ: a crafty white dog from Spitzbergen who leads the team

DAVE: a quiet dog who holds the wheeler position next to the sled

BILLEE: a friendly husky dog, Joe's brother

JOE: a mean husky dog, brother of Billee

SOL-LEKS: a one-eyed dog whose name means "Angry One"

CHARACTERS

PIKE, DUB AND DOLLY: three dogs added during the trek

TEEK AND KOONA: native huskies added at Rink Rapids

THE SCOTCH HALF-BREED: the mail carrier, Buck's second owner in the Klondike

CHARLES: an American tenderfoot in search of adventure, Buck's third owner in the Klondike

MERCEDES: Charles's wife

HAL: Mercedes's brother, the driver of the team

JOHN THORNTON: prospector in the Klondike who rescues Buck

NIGHT AND SKEET: John Thornton's dogs

HANS AND PETE: John Thornton's partners

"BLACK" BURTON: a bully in Dawson, Yukon

MATTHEWSON: a bragging man who makes a bet with Thornton

THE WILD BROTHER: a wild wolf who befriends Buck

THE YEEHATS: a native Indian tribe of the Yukon Territory

Chapter 1

A KIDNAPPED KING

Buck did not read the newspapers, or he would have known that trouble was ahead. Trouble not just for him but for every strong dog with warm, long hair along the western coastline. Men had found gold in the Arctic, and these men wanted dogs. The dogs they wanted were heavy dogs with strong muscles to pull dog sleds and with furry coats to protect them from the frost.

Buck lived at a big house in the sunny Santa Clara Valley. Judge Miller's place, it was called. It was a large, beautiful home with wrap-around porches and a long driveway. The estate had wide lawns with great stables, grape arbors, green pastures, orchards, and berry patches. Then there was the big cement tank where Judge Miller's boys took their morning swim and kept cool in the hot afternoon.

Buck ruled over this great estate. Here he was born, and here he had lived the four years of his life. There were other dogs, but they did not count. The house dogs and the kennel dogs came and went. But Buck was neither house dog nor kennel dog. The whole place was his. He jumped into the swimming tank, and went hunting with the Judge's sons. He went with Mollie and Alice, the Judge's daughters, on long walks. On wintry nights he lay at the Judge's feet before the roaring library fire. He carried the Judge's grandsons on his back, or rolled them in the grass, and played with them in the orchards. Buck was king—king over all the other dogs and every person at the Miller estate.

His father, Elmo, had been a huge St. Bernard, the Judge's favorite. Buck was not so large—he weighed only one hundred and forty pounds—for his mother, Shep, had been a Scotch shepherd dog. Nevertheless, he carried himself like a much larger dog, like the king he was, with great pride.

And this was the life Buck led in the fall of 1897, when the Klondike gold dragged men from all over the world into the frozen North. But Buck did not read the newspapers. He did not know that men's hearts could be turned with greed. Manuel, one of the gardener's helpers, *was* such a man whose heart had turned, and his greedy eyes had fallen on Buck—*a perfect sled dog.*

The Judge was at a meeting and the boys were at a club on the sad night of Manuel's crime. No one saw him take Buck and lead him through the orchard for an evening "stroll." And only one man saw them arrive at the little train station known as College Park. This one man talked with Manuel and handed him money.

"Are you going to tie him up?" the stranger asked gruffly.

Manuel doubled a piece of stout rope around Buck's neck under the collar. "Twist it, and you'll choke him plenty," said Manuel.

Buck did not resist the rope. He had learned to trust men he knew. But when the ends of the rope were placed in the stranger's hands, he growled to make the man let go. To his surprise, the rope tightened around his neck, shutting off his breath.

In a quick rage he sprang at the man, but the man was ready. He threw Buck onto his back and tightened the rope more. Never in all his life had Buck been so cruelly treated, and never in all his life had he been so angry. But his strength left him, his eyes closed, and he fainted from the rope and the pain. He was not even aware when the train came and the two men threw him into the baggage car.

The next he knew, he was being jolted along in something moving, and his tongue was hurting. The shriek of a train whistle told him where he was. He was kidnapped! He was a kidnapped king now full of anger. He opened his eyes and saw a man in the baggage car. The man's hand sprang to pull the rope, but Buck was too quick for him. His jaws closed on the hand—and he held on even as he was choked once again.

Later, in a small saloon, the man complained of his night's ride. "All I get is fifty dollars for this here dog," he grumbled, "and I wouldn't do it over for a *thousand* dollars!"

He held Buck firmly by the rope. The man's hand was wrapped up, and his pants were ripped from knee to ankle.

"How much did the other guy get?" the saloon-keeper asked.

"A hundred—wouldn't take a penny less."

"That makes a hundred and fifty dollars," the saloon-keeper said, "and he's worth it, or I don't know dogs. Here, lend me a hand with this brass collar he's wearing."

Dazed and in pain, Buck once more was thrown down and choked. The two men held him down as they filed his heavy brass collar from off his neck. Then the rope was removed, and he was flung into a cage-like crate. Without his collar, no one would ever know that he was the king of Judge Miller's estate.

There he lay for the rest of the night. He could not understand what it all meant. What did they want with him, these strange men? Why were they keeping him in this narrow crate? Several times during the night he sprang to his feet when the shed door rattled open, expecting to see the Judge, or the boys at least. But each time it was the ugly face of the saloon-keeper that looked in on him. And each time his hope turned into a savage growl.

In the morning, four men entered and picked up the crate—evil-looking men. Buck stormed and raged at them through the bars. They only laughed and poked sticks at him as the crate was lifted into a wagon. Then Buck began a long journey—on a wagon, a truck, a ferry steamer, and finally on yet another train—passing through many hands to a place he knew not where.

Chapter 2

THE LAW OF CLUB

For two days and nights Buck neither ate nor drank. Shaking, he flung himself against the bars. The hunger was painful, but the thirst for water was torture. His throat was dry, his tongue was swollen, and his body burned with fever.

He was glad for one thing—the rope was off his neck. Never again would a man get a rope around his neck. For in those two days and nights of torment, he was changed into a new animal—a raging beast. He was so changed that the Judge himself would not have recognized him. The train workers were glad to see this fierce beast leave the train at Seattle.

Four men carefully carried the crate from the wagon into a small yard. A stout man with a red sweater came out and signed the book for the driver. Buck knew this was the next tormentor and he hurled himself against the bars. The man smiled grimly, and brought out a hatchet and a club.

"You ain't going to take him out *now*?" the driver asked.

"Sure," the man replied, prying the crate open with the hatchet.

The four men, who had carried the crate in, quickly scattered and got atop a safe, high wall to watch.

Buck snarled, growled, and rushed at the sides of the crate.

"Now, you red-eyed devil," said the man in the red sweater, when the crate was dashed open. He dropped the hatchet and shifted the club to his right hand.

And Buck truly *was* a red-eyed devil—with hair bristling, mouth foaming, a mad glitter in his bloodshot eyes. Straight at the man he launched his one hundred and forty pounds of fury. In mid-air, just as his jaws were about to close on the man,

he received a shocking blow. He whirled over, hitting the ground on his back and side. He had never been struck by a club in his life and did not understand. With a snarl that was part bark and more scream, he was again on his feet and he launched into the air. And again the shock came and he was brought crushingly to the ground. This time he knew it was the club, but a dozen times he charged, and a dozen times the club broke the charge and smashed him down.

Buck crawled to his feet, too dazed to rush. He staggered limply about, the blood flowing from nose and mouth and ears. Then the man gave him a frightful blow on the nose. All the pain he had ever known was nothing compared with this. With a lion-like roar, he again hurled himself at the man. The man struck a final blow and Buck crumpled up and went down, knocked completely senseless.

"He can break a dog, that's what I say," one of the men on the wall exclaimed.

"I'd rather break wild mustangs any day," was the reply of the driver, as he climbed on the wagon and started the horses.

Buck's senses came back to him, but not his strength. He lay where he had fallen, and from there he watched the man in the red sweater.

The man read over the note that came with the crate.

"Well, Buck, my boy," he went on in a friendly voice, "we've had our little lesson, and the best thing we can do is to let it go at that. You've learned your place, and I know mine. Be a good dog and all will go well. Be a bad dog, and I'll beat the stuffing outa you. Understand?"

As he spoke he patted the head he had so cruelly pounded with no mercy. Buck's hair bristled at the touch of the hand, but he lay still. When the man brought him water, he drank eagerly, and later gulped down a meal of raw meat, chunk by chunk, from the man's hand.

He was beaten (he knew that), but he was not broken. He saw that he stood no chance against a man with a club. He had learned the lesson, and he would never forget it.

As the days went by, other dogs came, in crates and at the ends of ropes. Some came quietly, and some raged and roared.

Buck watched each new dog pass under the club of the man in the red sweater. And he knew then that a man with a club was a lawgiver, a master to be obeyed—but never a friend.

More strangers came who talked quietly and eagerly to the man in the red sweater. Money passed between them and the strangers took one or more of the dogs away with them. Buck wondered where they went, for they never came back.

And then *his* time came. A little wrinkled man who spoke broken English spotted Buck.

"*Ola!*" he cried, when his eyes lit upon Buck. "Dat one bully dog! Eh? How much?"

"Three hundred, and that is a bargain," said the man in the red sweater. "And you are paying with government money. You can afford that, eh, Perrault?"

Perrault grinned. For so fine an animal this was not a high price. The Canadian Government could well afford such a dog. Perrault knew dogs, and when he looked at Buck he knew that he was one in a thousand—"One in ten thousand," he said to himself.

Buck saw money pass between them. Perrault also bought another dog—a good-natured Newfoundland named Curly—and he led the two dogs away. That was the last Buck saw of the man in the red sweater.

As Curly and he looked at the shoreline from the deck of the boat, it was the last he saw of the warm land of the Southland coast.

Chapter 3

THE LAW OF FANG

Curly and Buck were taken below deck by Perrault and handed over to a large man called François. Both men were French Canadian, tan and weathered from Klondike life. This was a new kind of man to Buck. He did not befriend them, but he grew to respect them. He soon learned that Perrault and François were fair men, but too wise in the way of dogs to be fooled by dogs.

Between decks, Buck and Curly joined two other dogs. One was a big, snow-white fellow from Spitzbergen who had been brought away by a whaling captain. He was friendly—but not to be trusted. "Spitz," as he was called, would smile

while he planned some sneaky trick—and he indeed proved himself to be sneaky. When he stole from Buck's food at the first meal, Buck sprang to punish him. Just then the lash of François's whip sang through the air, reaching the white dog first. Buck observed that this at least was fair treatment from this man with the whip.

The other dog was called "Dave." He was a quiet fellow who wanted to be left alone. His eyes told the others that there would be trouble if he were bothered. When the boat rolled and pitched, Buck and Curly became half-wild with fear. But Dave merely raised his head as though annoyed, glanced their way, yawned, and went to sleep again.

At last one morning the boat came to a stop. The excitement of change was in the air. François leashed the dogs and brought them on deck. At the first step upon the cold deck, Buck's feet sank into a white mushy something very like mud. He sprang back with a snort. More of this white stuff was falling through the air. He shook himself, but more of it fell upon him. He sniffed it curiously, then licked some up on his tongue. It bit like fire, and the next instant was gone. This puzzled him. He tried it again, with the same results. The men laughed, and he felt ashamed. This was the first time he had ever seen snow.

Buck's first day on the shore was like a nightmare. Every hour was filled with shock and surprise. No lazy, sunny life was this. Here there was no peace, nor rest, nor a moment's safety— only confusion and danger. Buck knew he must stay alert. These dogs and men were not town dogs and men. They were savages, all of them. They knew no law but the law of club and fang.

He had never seen dogs fight as these wolfish dogs fought. Buck soon learned an awful lesson about life in these wild parts—and Curly, the Newfoundland, was the victim.

The Call of the Wild

They were camped near the log store, where Curly, in her friendly way, walked up to a husky dog the size of a full-grown wolf. With no warning, the husky leaped in like a flash, sank his teeth into Curly, then leaped back—almost in one motion.

It was the wolf way of fighting. Strike and leap away. Yet there was more to the wolf way than this. Thirty or forty huskies ran to the spot and surrounded the two dogs in a silent circle. Buck did not understand this silent circle, nor why they were licking their chops. Curly rushed the husky, who struck again and leaped aside. He met her next rush with his chest and tumbled her off her feet. She never got back up. This was what the circle of huskies had waited for. They closed in upon her, snarling and yelping in a mass attack. Within seconds, Curly was dead.

Buck was shocked by this sudden, brutal act. He saw Spitz stick out his red tongue in a way he had of laughing. Then he saw François, swinging an axe, spring into the mess of dogs. Three men with clubs were helping him to scatter them. It did not take long. The wild huskies were driven off and there lay Curly, limp and lifeless in the snow.

This memory often came back to Buck to trouble him in his sleep. So that was the way. No fair play. Once down, that was the end of you. Well, he would see to it that he never went down. Spitz stuck out his tongue and laughed again. From that moment Buck hated him with a bitter and deep hatred.

---------- *Chapter 4* ----------

THE TEAM

Before long, Buck received another shock. François walked over to him with something made of leather straps. He then buckled and fastened this upon Buck. It was a harness.

Buck had often seen such harnesses put on horses back home on Judge Miller's estate. These horses were then put to work—something Buck had never been made to do. Yet now he was set to work pulling François on a sled to the forest for a load of firewood.

Buck had become a work animal. His pride suffered a blow. And though this was new and strange, he was determined to do his best.

Buck became the middle member of the three-dog sled team. He soon learned that order and teamwork were necessary. François was stern and taught the dogs to obey with his whip. Dave had worked on a team before and was an experienced "wheeler," holding the position closest to the sled. He nipped at Buck's hind legs whenever he was in error. Spitz was the lead dog. He growled sharply now and again and threw his weight into the two straps—the "traces"—that linked all the dogs.

Buck learned easily, and made good progress. Before they returned to camp, he knew enough to stop at "Ho," to go ahead at "Mush," to swing wide on the bends, and to keep clear of the wheeler when the loaded sled shot downhill at their heels.

"Three very good dogs," François told Perrault. "Dat Buck, him can pull! I teach him quick as anything."

By afternoon, Perrault returned with two more dogs. "Billee" and "Joe" he called them. They were brothers, and true huskies both, yet different as day and night. Billee was very friendly while Joe was sour and silent with an evil eye. Buck was friendly to both dogs and Dave ignored them. Spitz wanted to prove who was leader from the start. When Billee wagged his tail at Spitz, the white dog attacked him, sinking sharp teeth into the husky's flank. Then Spitz circled Joe. Billee had fled, but Joe whirled around on his heels to face Spitz—ears laid back, lips snarling, jaws clipping together, and eyes gleaming with stubborn fear.

By evening Perrault brought another dog, an old thin husky with only one good eye. He was called Sol-leks, which means "Angry One." Like Dave, he asked nothing, gave nothing, and commanded respect. Even Spitz left him alone. Sol-leks did not like to be approached on his blind side. Buck was unlucky enough to discover this. Sol-leks whirled upon Buck and slashed his shoulder to the bone when Buck walked up to the side with the bad eye. After this, Buck avoided his blind side, and had no more trouble.

That night Buck faced the great problem of sleeping out in the freezing cold. The tent was lit by a candle and it glowed warmly. Buck walked into the warm tent, but both Perrault and François yelled and threw plates and cups at him till he fled into the outer cold. He lay down on the snow and attempted to sleep, but he was shivering. Sadly he wandered about among the many tents. Each place was as cold as another.

Finally an idea came to him. He would return and see how his own teammates were making out. To his surprise, they had disappeared. Again he wandered about through the great camp, looking for them, and again he returned. Were they in the tent? No, that could not be, else he would not have been driven out. Then where could they possibly be? With drooping tail and shivering body he circled the tent. Suddenly the snow gave way beneath his forelegs and he sank down. Something wriggled under his feet. He sprang back, bristling and snarling. But a friendly little yelp calmed him and brought him back. There, curled up under the snow in a snug ball, lay Billee. He whined, squirmed, and wriggled to show his good will, and even licked Buck's face with his warm, wet tongue.

THE CALL OF THE WILD

Another lesson. So that was the way they did it, eh? Buck selected a spot and, after a few tries, finally dug a hole for himself. The day had been long and hard. He slept soundly and comfortably, though he growled and barked and wrestled with bad dreams.

Buck did not open his eyes until he heard the sounds of the waking camp. At first he did not know where he was. It had snowed during the night and he was completely buried. The muscles of his whole body ached. The hair on his neck and shoulders stood on end. With a ferocious snarl, he bounded straight up into the open air, sending the snow flying. He landed on his feet and saw the camp. Then he remembered everything that had happened to him—from the stroll with Manuel, to the boat ride, to the sled team, to the hole he had dug for himself the night before.

"What I say?" the dog-driver François cried to Perrault. "Dat Buck for sure learn quick as anything."

Perrault nodded. The Canadian Government needed the best dogs on this run. He was glad to have Buck.

THE CALL OF THE WILD

JACK LONDON

Three more huskies were added to the team, making a total of nine. Before long they were in harness and swinging up the trail away from the camp. Buck was glad to be gone. The work was hard, but he did not hate it. He was surprised at how much the other dogs enjoyed the work. They were all eager to get down the trail.

Dave was wheeler, or sled dog. Pulling in front of him was Buck. Then came Sol-leks. The rest of the team was strung out ahead, single file, to the leader—Spitz. Buck had been placed between Dave and Sol-leks to be taught the way of the team. When he needed instruction, he received a sharp nip or a pull in the traces.

That day they made forty miles on the snow-packed trail. The next few days they had to blaze a new trail, which was harder work and took more time. Perrault traveled ahead of the team, packing the snow with webbed shoes to make it easier for them. François usually guided the sled with the gee-pole. Perrault was in a hurry, but he knew the danger in rushing onto the thin autumn ice.

Day after day, Buck toiled in the traces. Always they broke camp in the dark of the early hours. At the first gray of dawn they were hitting the trail.

THE CALL OF THE WILD

After dark the men pitched camp. The dogs ate their bit of fish, and crawled to sleep into the snow. Buck was starving. His pound and a half of sun-dried salmon was not enough food for his aching belly. The other dogs weighed less and were born to this life. A pound only of the fish kept them in good condition.

Buck watched and learned. When he saw Pike, one of the new dogs, slyly steal a slice of bacon when Perrault's back was turned, he copied the trick the following day, getting away with the whole chunk. An uproar was raised, but Buck was not suspected. Dub, who was always getting caught, was blamed and punished for Buck's misdeed.

Buck quickly grew strong and wise. His muscles became as hard as iron and he grew used to pain. He could eat anything, no matter how disgusting. He learned to bite the ice out with his teeth when it collected between his toes. When he was thirsty and the ice was thick over a water hole, he would strike and break it with stiff forelegs. His sense of smell and sense of hearing became very keen. His instincts came alive within him—the instincts of the wild, the instincts of his nature.

On the quiet, cold nights, he pointed his nose at a star and howled long and wolf-like. The "old song" of his ancient ancestors ran through him and he began to discover the primitive beast within him—a Buck he never knew—a Buck that had come alive all because men had found gold in the North, and because Manuel was a greedy man.

Chapter 5 ———

THE PRIMITIVE BEAST

The "primitive beast" was strong in Buck
and his life on the trail made it more and more
dominant. He became cunning, with great poise
and intelligence. He did not pick fights and
he avoided them whenever possible. Even
though he hated Spitz, he remained in control
of his actions.

On the other hand, Spitz was always showing
his teeth. He bullied Buck, trying to start the
fight that could end only in the death of one or
the other.

At the end of one hard day, they set up
a quick camp on the shore of Lake Le Barge.

The wind cut like a white-hot knife. Darkness and the driving snow forced them to search for a camping place.

Under a sheltering rock, Buck made his nest in the snow. It was so snug and warm that he hated to leave it when François brought out a dinner of thawed fish. But when Buck finished his meal and returned, he found his nest occupied. There came a snarl from the trespasser—it was Spitz! Till now Buck had avoided trouble with his enemy, but this was too much. The beast in him roared. He sprang upon Spitz with a fury that surprised them both.

François was surprised, too, when both men rushed out to see the cause of the trouble.

"A-a-ah!" he cried to cheer on Buck. "Gif it to him! Gif it to him, the dirty thief!"

Spitz and Buck were circling each other with rage and caution. Then—suddenly—something happened that stopped the fight.

Perrault cried out and Buck heard the sound of a club and a shrill yelp of pain. The camp was alive with strange furry forms—a pack of starving huskies! There were eighty to one hundred of them. They had smelled the camp from some Indian village and were crazed by the smell of food.

In an instant the skinny brutes scrambled for the bread and bacon in a grub box. The men used their clubs with no effect. The wild dogs yelped and howled under the blows, but struggled madly till the last crumb was devoured.

The sled dogs burst out of their nests, only to be attacked by the fierce wild huskies. Never had Buck seen such dogs. They were like skeletons, with blazing eyes and frothing fangs, leaping toward the sled dogs. Buck's head and shoulders were ripped and slashed. Billee was crying as usual. Dave and Sol-leks dripped with blood, fighting bravely side by side. Joe snapped fiercely upon an invader's leg. Pike finished the job. Buck flung himself upon one, then another, till he felt teeth sink into his own throat. It was Spitz, attacking him from the side.

Perrault and François hurried to save their sled dogs. The wild, starving beasts fled and Buck shook himself free of Spitz. But it was only for a moment. The men then ran back to save the rest of the grub, and the huskies returned to attack the team. Billee sprang through the savage circle and fled away over the ice. Pike and Dub followed on his heels, with the rest of the team behind.

THE CALL OF THE WILD

As Buck drew himself together to spring after them, out of the corner of his eye he saw Spitz rush upon him. He took the brunt of Spitz's charge, then joined the flight out on the frozen lake.

Later, the nine team-dogs gathered together in the forest. There was not one who was not wounded in four or five places. Dub was badly injured in a hind leg. Dolly, the last husky added to the team, had a badly torn throat. Joe had lost an eye. The good-natured Billee, with a ripped ear, cried and whimpered throughout the night. At daybreak they limped back to camp. The wild huskies had fled and the two men were in bad moods. Half their grub supply was gone. The huskies had chewed through the sled lashings. They had eaten a pair of Perrault's moose-hide moccasins, chunks out of the leather traces, and even two feet of lash from the end of François's whip. He looked up from the mess to see to his wounded dogs—wounded with the bites of huskies gone mad.

"Ah, my friends," he said softly, "mebbe it make you mad dog, those many bites. Mebbe all mad dog! What you think, eh, Perrault?"

Perrault shook his head. With four hundred miles of trail still between him and Dawson, he could not afford to have madness break out among his dogs. Two hours and much hard work later, the harnesses were repaired and the wounded team was underway. The hardest part of the trail between them and Dawson lay before them.

Chapter 6

THE FIGHT

It took six days of toil to cover thirty terrible miles. A dozen times Perrault, nosing the way, broke through the ice, being saved by the long pole he carried. Each time he broke through, he had to quickly build a fire to dry his garments. Once, the sled broke through—pulling Dave and Buck with it. They were half-frozen and all but drowned by the time they were dragged out. At another time Spitz went through, dragging the whole team after him up to Buck, who strained backward with all his strength. Behind him was Dave, straining backward, and behind the sled was François, pulling till his tendons cracked.

JACK LONDON

THE CALL OF THE WILD

JACK LONDON

The entire team became exhausted. Perrault, to make up lost time, still pushed the tired dogs late and early.

Buck's feet were not so compact and hard as the feet of the huskies. All day long he limped in pain. At camp he lay down like a dead dog. He could not even move to get his dinner. François had to bring it to him. Perrault rubbed Buck's feet for half an hour each night after supper. He cut off the tops of his own moccasins to make four moccasins for Buck. This was a great relief. One morning François forgot the moccasins and Buck lay on his back, his four feet waving in the air. Perrault grinned at the sight of a dog that refused to budge without his "shoes." Later Buck's feet grew hard to the trail, and the worn-out footgear was thrown away.

One morning as they were harnessing up, Dolly went suddenly mad. Her long, sad wolf howl sent every dog bristling with fear. She then sprang straight for Buck. He had never seen a dog go mad, and he fled in a panic. Dolly, foaming at the mouth, ran wildly after Buck. At François's call, Buck circled back into camp. Here, the dog-driver waited with the axe which he brought down on the crazed, sick Dolly.

Buck staggered over to the sled, exhausted, sobbing for breath. This was Spitz's opportunity. He sprang upon Buck, and twice his teeth sank in and ripped the flesh to the bone. Then François's lash cracked, and Buck watched Spitz receive the worst whipping as yet given to any of the team.

"One devil, dat Spitz," remarked Perrault. "Some day him kill dat Buck."

"Dat Buck is two devils," was François's reply. "All de time I watch dat Buck, I know for sure. Listen… some fine day him get angry and den him chew dat Spitz all up. Sure, I know."

From then on it was war between Buck and Spitz. Spitz, as lead dog, had battled many dogs before. But Buck was different—he was smarter and more patient. Buck wanted the leadership position. He wanted it because it was his nature. He wanted it because he was gripped with a pride that matched the pride of Spitz.

One morning after a heavy snowfall, Pike did not appear. He was hidden in his nest under a foot of snow. François called for him but he still did not come. Spitz was wild with anger that a dog would disobey. He raged through the camp, smelling and digging until he found Pike in his hiding place.

Spitz flew at Pike to punish him. Just then, Buck flew with equal rage in between. Surprised, Spitz was hurled backward and off his feet. Pike joined the fight and Buck also sprang upon Spitz. But François, chuckling at the fight, brought his lash down upon Buck with all his might. Half-stunned, Buck was knocked backward and the lash fell upon him again and again, while Spitz soundly punished Pike.

In the days that followed, as Dawson grew closer and closer, Buck continued to interfere between Spitz and the other dogs. But he was crafty, waiting until François was not around. The team went from bad to worse. Things no longer went right. There was constant nipping and yelping—and at the bottom of it all was Buck. He kept François busy, watching out for the life-and-death struggle between Spitz and Buck that he knew would take place sooner or later.

They pulled into Dawson one dreary afternoon with the great fight still to come. Here were many men and countless dogs, all at work. All day they swung up and down the main street in long teams, and in the night their jingling bells still went by.

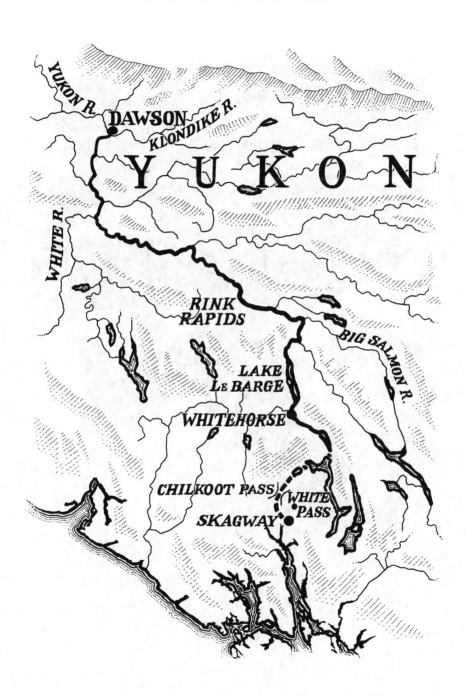

Here and there Buck met Southland dogs, like himself, but most were the wild wolf-husky breed. Every night, regularly at nine, at twelve, and three, they howled the eerie "old song." Buck joined them—the new Buck—the primordial beast.

The team rested for a day, then got back on the trail. They made splendid progress, but Buck kept stirring up trouble along the way. They no longer worked as "one dog" in the traces. Spitz was no longer a leader who was feared or respected. Pike robbed him of half a fish one night, and gulped it down under the protection of Buck. Another night Dub and Joe fought Spitz and watched him take the punishment that *they* deserved. And even Billee, the good-natured, grew more brave. Buck never came near Spitz without snarling and bristling.

François became furious with the team. His lash was always singing among the dogs, but it did little good. When his back was turned the dogs were at it again. François knew Buck was behind all of the trouble, and Buck knew François knew. Buck was too clever to ever again be caught red-handed.

One night after supper, Dub turned up a snowshoe rabbit and in a second the whole team was in full cry. A hundred yards away was a camp of the Northwest Police, with fifty huskies who joined the rabbit-chase. The rabbit sped down the river and turned off into a small creek, up the frozen bed. Buck led the pack, sixty strong, around bend after bend, but he could not gain. His splendid body flashed forward, leap by leap, in the pale white moonlight. And leap by leap the snowshoe rabbit flashed on ahead. Buck still led the pack, running the wild thing down.

But Spitz, cold and crafty, left the pack and cut across a piece of land along the creek. Buck did not know of this. As Buck rounded the bend, he saw a large, frosty shadow leap into the path of the rabbit. It was Spitz! The rabbit could not turn, and Spitz's white teeth seized it.

Buck made no sound, but drove in upon Spitz, shoulder to shoulder, so hard that he missed the throat. They rolled over and over in the powdery snow. Spitz gained his feet almost as though he had not been overthrown, slashing Buck's shoulder and leaping clear.

In a flash Buck knew it. The time had come. It was to the death. As they circled about, snarling, ears laid back, Buck's instincts took over. He seemed to remember it all—the white woods, and earth, and moonlight, and the thrill of battle. The air was silent and the wolf-huskies circled, their eyes gleaming.

Spitz knew how to fight, and whenever Buck lunged he was met with quicker fangs. Time and time again he leaped at Spitz, and each time Spitz slashed him and got away. Spitz was untouched, while Buck was streaming with blood and panting hard. The fight was growing desperate. Once Buck flipped over, and the whole circle of sixty dogs started up. But he recovered himself, almost in midair, and the circle sank down again… and waited.

Buck was smart—smarter than any dog Spitz had known. He rushed, pretending to go for the shoulder, but at the last instant he swept in low and closed on Spitz's left foreleg. The bone broke—and the white dog faced him on three legs. Buck tried again to knock him over, and then swept in to break the right foreleg. Despite the pain and helplessness, Spitz struggled to keep up.

THE CALL OF THE WILD

But there was no hope for Spitz, and no mercy.

Buck readied for the final rush. A pause seemed to fall. Every animal stood still as though turned to stone. Then Buck sprang in— delivered the final bite—and sprang out. No more would Spitz stand in his way. Buck was again a king.

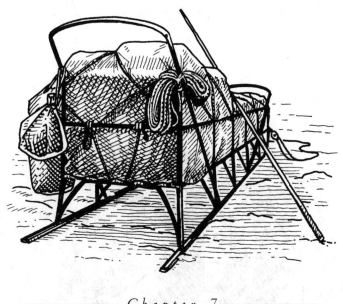

Chapter 7

WHO WILL LEAD?

"Eh? What I say? I speak true when I say dat Buck two devils," said François the next morning.

"Dat Spitz fight like the devil," said Perrault, as he looked over the rips and cuts.

"An' dat Buck fight like *two* devils," was François's answer. "And now we make good time. No more Spitz, no more trouble, sure."

Perrault packed up and loaded the sled while François started to harness the dogs. Buck trotted up to the place Spitz used to hold as leader. François, not noticing him, brought Sol-leks to the lead. Buck sprang upon Sol-leks in a fury, driving him back and standing in his place.

"Eh? Eh?" François cried, slapping his thighs gleefully. "Look at dat Buck. Him kill dat Spitz, him think to take de job. Go 'way, now, Buck!"

Buck refused to budge.

He took Buck by the scruff of the neck, dragged him to one side, and put Sol-leks back in the lead. The old dog did not like it—he was afraid of Buck. When François turned his back, Buck again made Sol-leks step aside.

François was angry. "Now, by darn, I fix you!" he cried, coming back with a heavy club in his hand.

Buck remembered the man in the red sweater, and backed away slowly. He did not charge in when Sol-leks was once more put in the lead. He circled, just beyond reach of the club, snarling with rage.

The driver went about his work. He called to Buck when he was ready to put him in his old place in front of Dave. Buck took two or three steps back. François followed him up. Buck retreated again. After some time of this, François threw down the club, thinking that Buck feared a thrashing. But Buck was in open revolt. He wanted to be the leader. It was his by right.

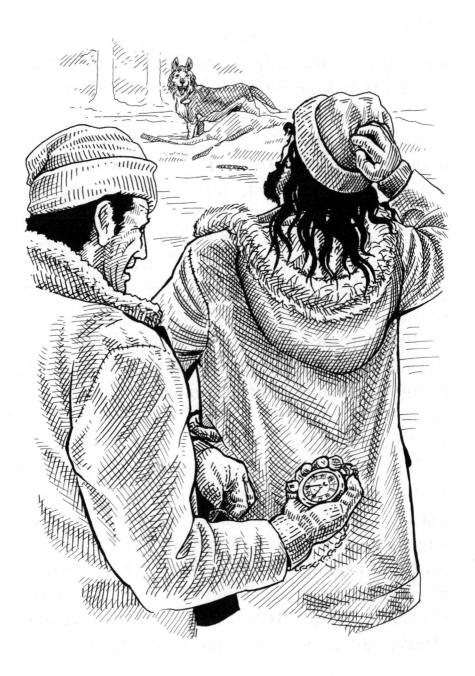

He had earned it, and he would not be content with less.

Perrault came to help, but for an hour the two men could not get Buck into position. They threw clubs at him. He dodged. They yelled at him, and he snarled and kept out of their reach. He did not try to run away, but retreated around and around the camp.

François sat down and scratched his head. Perrault angrily looked at his watch. Time was flying. They should have been on the trail an hour ago. François scratched his head again. He shook it and grinned at Perrault, who shrugged his shoulders. Then François went up to where Sol-leks stood and called to Buck. Buck laughed, as dogs laugh, yet kept his distance. François unfastened Sol-leks's traces and put him back in his old place. The team stood harnessed and ready for the trail, with only one open spot—the lead position.

François called and Buck trotted in, laughing in triumph. He swung around into position at the head of the team. His traces were fastened, the sled was broken out, and with both men running they dashed out onto the river trail.

Buck proved to be an excellent leader. He kept order among the dogs and kept the team moving at a fast pace. Dave and Sol-leks did not mind the change in leadership. They loved the work—the toil in the traces—and Buck worked them hard. The rest of the team had grown unruly during Spitz's last days, and they were surprised at how Buck got them all into shape.

Pike, who pulled at Buck's heels, was used to being lazy. Buck swiftly punished him, and, before the first day was done, Pike was pulling more than ever before in his life. The first night in camp, Joe, the sour one, was disciplined with bites and snarls. Buck let the team know who was boss—and the team improved greatly. Once more the dogs leaped as "one dog" in the traces.

At the Rink Rapids, two native huskies—Teek and Koona—were added. Buck broke them so quickly it took away François's breath.

"Never such a dog as dat Buck!" he cried. "No, never! Him worth one thousand dollars, for sure! Eh? What you say, Perrault?"

And Perrault nodded. He was ahead of the record then, and gaining day by day. The trail was in excellent condition, well packed and hard.

JACK LONDON

There was no new soft snow, and it was not too cold. The men rode and ran by turn, and the dogs were kept on the jump. On the last night of the second week, they topped White Pass and dropped down the sea slope toward Skagway.

It was a record run. Each day for fourteen days they had averaged forty miles. When they reached Skagway, the team became the center of attention by a crowd of dogbusters and mushers.

The mission was now complete. The two Canadians had new orders that required a fresh team of dogs. François called Buck to him, threw his arms around him, and wept good-bye. And that was the last of François and Perrault. Like other men, they passed out of Buck's life for good.

Chapter 8

THE TOIL OF THE TRAIL

A mail carrier, a Scotch half-breed, took charge of Buck's team, along with a dozen other dog teams. The sleds were loaded up with sacks of mail, and the dogs started back over the weary trail to Dawson. The running was hard now. The loads were heavy. There was toil each day. There were no record times.

Buck did not like it, but he pulled hard and took pride in his work—just like Dave and Solleks did. As leader, he made sure that every dog did his fair share of the work.

It was a boring life. One day was very much like another. At a certain time each morning,

the cooks turned out, fires were built, and breakfast was eaten. Then, while some broke camp, others harnessed the dogs, and they were underway an hour or so before dawn. At night, camp was made. Some pitched the tents, others cut firewood and collected pine branches for the beds. Still others carried water or ice for the cooks. Then the dogs were fed their meal of fish. This was the one time of day when the team could relax for an hour or so with the other dogs.

Best of all, Buck loved to lie near the fire with his eyes blinking dreamily at the flames. Sometimes he thought of Judge Miller's big house in the sunny Santa Clara Valley, and of the swimming tank. But more often he remembered the man in the red sweater, the death of Curly, the great fight with Spitz, and the good things he had eaten or would like to eat. He was not homesick. His old home was a very dim and distant memory. Far more powerful were his instincts. These new instincts seemed to come from ancestors long ago—from a time when the dog was a wild breed running with a wilder sort of man.

Sometimes as he crouched there, blinking at the flames, it seemed that the flames were of another fire. As if in a dream, he saw a different man from the Canadian cook in front of him. This other man had short, muscular legs and long arms. The hair was long and matted. He uttered strange sounds, and seemed very much afraid of the darkness as he peered into it. He clutched a stick with a heavy stone at one end. He was a hairy, primitive man—a primordial man. He did not stand up straight, but leaned forward from the hips on legs that bent at the knees—as if ready to pounce out of fear.

At other times this hairy man squatted by the fire with his head between his legs and slept. And beyond that fire, in the darkness, Buck could see many gleaming eyes, always two by two, which he knew to be the eyes of great beasts of prey. And he could hear the crashing of their bodies through the undergrowth, and the noises they made in the night.

These sounds and sights of this dream-like world would make the hair rise along his back. He would whimper low or growl softly, and the cook would shout at him, "Hey, you Buck, wake up!"

THE CALL OF THE WILD

Then the other world would vanish and the real world would come into his eyes. He would get up and yawn and stretch as though he had been asleep.

The loads of mail were heavy and this was a hard trip. The work wore the dogs down. They were in poor condition when they finally pulled into Dawson, and should have had a week-long rest. But within two days' time they were loaded up again to take more mail loads. The dogs were tired, the drivers grumbled, and, to make matters worse, it snowed every day. This meant a soft trail and heavier pulling for the dogs. The drivers were fair through it all, and did their best for the dogs.

Each night the dogs were attended to first. They ate before the drivers ate, and no man went to sleep without first checking on the feet of the dogs he drove. Still, their strength went down. Since the beginning of the winter, they had traveled nearly 2000 miles, dragging sleds the whole weary distance. Buck stood it, leading his team well, though he too was very tired. Billee cried and whimpered in his sleep each night. Joe was more sour than ever, and Sol-leks only wanted to be left alone.

But it was Dave who suffered most of all. He became more sad and irritable. When camp was pitched, he made his nest at once, where his driver fed him. He did not get on his feet again till harness-up time in the morning. He often cried out in pain in the traces. The driver examined him, but could find nothing. All the drivers became interested in his case. They talked it over at meal time. He was brought from his nest to the fire and was pressed and prodded till he cried out many times. Something was wrong inside him, but they could find no broken bones.

By the time they reached Cassiar Bar, he was so weak that again and again he fell in the traces. The Scotch mail carrier called a halt and took him out of the team, making the next dog, Sol-leks, the new wheeler next to the sled. He wanted to give Dave a rest and let him run free behind the sled. Sick as he was, Dave would have no part of this. He growled while his traces were removed. He whimpered broken-heartedly when he saw Sol-leks in the position he had held and served so long. His pride was hurt—and this was more painful than his illness. He could not bear that another dog should do his work.

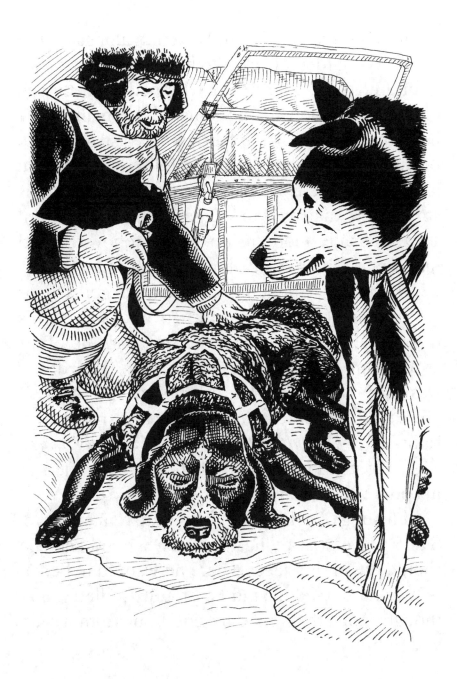

When the sled started, Dave ran alongside the team, trying to get back into his place, crying with grief and pain. The driver whipped him, but he paid no attention to the stings. The man didn't have the heart to strike harder. Dave struggled to run behind the sled. Then he fell howling as the long train of sleds went by. With the last bit of his strength he managed to stagger along behind until the train made another stop. He somehow reached his own sled and stood alongside Sol-leks.

His driver stopped a moment to get a light for his pipe. Then he returned and started his dogs. They swung out on the trail with no effort at all—but then stopped in surprise. The driver was surprised, too. The sled had not moved! He called the other men over to see the strange sight. *Dave had bitten through both of Sol-leks' traces*, and was standing directly in front of the sled in his proper place.

The dog pleaded with his eyes to remain there. Since Dave was dying, the men agreed that he should die in the traces where he wanted to be. So he was harnessed in, and he proudly pulled again, though more than once he cried out from a pain within him.

He held out till camp was reached and his driver made a place for him by the fire. In the morning he was too weak to travel. His strength had left him and he was dying. He could not be harnessed, and the team went on without him. The whips snapped, the bells jingled merrily, the sleds churned along the trail.

Buck knew, and every dog knew, they would never see Dave again.

Chapter 9

THE TENDERFEET

Thirty days from the time they left Dawson, Buck and his team arrived at Skagway. They were worn out and worn down. Buck's one hundred and forty pounds had gone down to one hundred and fifteen. The rest of his mates had lost weight, too. Pike limped with a hurt leg. Sol-leks was also limping, and Dub was suffering from a hurt shoulder blade. The dogs were all very footsore. Their feet plodded along with no joy for the work. The months of constant toil left them with no strength. It had all been used. Every muscle, every fiber, every cell was tired—dead tired. And there was reason for it.

In less than five months they had traveled 2500 miles with little or no rest. When they arrived at Skagway, they were on their last legs.

"Mush on, poor sore feets," the driver said as they slowly staggered down the main street of Skagway. "This is de last. Then we get one long rest, eh? For sure. One long rest."

The drivers expected a long stopover. They deserved a rest and a chance to relax. But there were so many men who had rushed to the Klondike in search of gold that the mail loads had increased. Fresh teams of dogs were brought in to take the places of the worn-out teams. These worthless dog teams were no longer useful on the mail runs—and so these teams were sold.

After only three days of rest, Buck's team—harness and all—was bought by two men from the United States. The men called each other "Hal" and "Charles." Charles was a man about age forty, with watery eyes and a mustache that twisted up. Hal was a young man of nineteen or twenty, with a big revolver and a hunting knife strapped to his belt. Both men were out of place. They were "Tenderfeet"—newcomers who did not know the ways of the wild North.

The new owners' camp was a mess. The tent was put up poorly and the dishes were not washed. There was also a woman with them called "Mercedes." She was Charles's wife and Hal's sister. Three Tenderfeet in one family.

Buck watched the two men take the camp apart and load the sled. They did not know how to roll the tent. The tin dishes were packed away unwashed. Mercedes kept complaining and giving advice to Hal and Charles. They packed and unpacked several times, never getting things "just right" for Mercedes.

Three men from a neighboring tent came out and looked on, grinning and winking at one another.

"You've got a right big load as it is," said one of them. "It's not for me to say, but I wouldn't tote that tent along if I was you."

"Nonsense!" cried Mercedes. "However in the world could I manage without a tent?"

"It's springtime, ma'am, and you won't get any more cold weather," the man replied.

She shook her head at the men.

"Ya think that sled will ride?" one of the men asked.

"Why shouldn't it?" Charles demanded.

"I was just a-wondering, that is all. It seemed a mite top-heavy," said the man.

Charles turned his back and tied the bundles down as best he could—which was rather sloppily.

"And of course the dogs can hike all day with that top-heavy load, eh?" came another comment.

"Certainly," said Hal. He took hold of the gee-pole with one hand and the whip with the other. "Mush!" he shouted. "Mush on there!"

The dogs sprang forward, strained hard for a few moments, then relaxed. They were unable to move the sled.

"The lazy brutes! I'll show them," Hal cried, raising his whip.

But Mercedes cried, "Oh, Hal, you mustn't!" She caught hold of the whip and pulled it from him. "The poor dears! Now you must promise you won't be harsh with them for the rest of the trip, or I won't go a step."

"You know nothing about dogs," her brother sneered, "and I wish you'd leave me alone. They're lazy, I tell you, and you've got to whip them to get anything out of them. That's their way. You ask anyone. Ask one of those men."

THE CALL OF THE WILD

Mercedes looked at the men.

"They're much too weak, if you want to know," replied one. "Plumb tuckered out, that's what's the matter. They need a rest."

"Rest indeed," snarled Hal.

"Never mind that man," Mercedes said. "You're driving our dogs and you do what you think best with them."

Again Hal's whip fell upon the dogs. They threw themselves forward, dug their feet into the packed snow, got down low to it, and put forth all their strength. The sled would not move. After two efforts, they stood still, panting. Hal's whip kept singing. Mercedes stopped the whipping, dropped on her knees before Buck, and with tears in her eyes, put her arms around his neck.

"You poor, poor dears," she cried, "why don't you pull hard? Then you wouldn't be whipped."

Buck did not like her.

An onlooker spoke up. "I don't care a whoop what becomes of *you*, but for the dogs' sakes I just want to tell you this. You can help them a mighty lot by breaking out that sled. The runners are frozen in the icy snow. Throw your weight against the gee-pole, right and left, and *break* it out."

After a third try, Hal broke out the runners which had been frozen in the snow. The dogs managed to pull the overloaded sled down the path. But when the path turned onto the main street, the top-heavy sled went over, spilling half its load.

The dogs never stopped—the sled bounded on its side behind them. Buck was raging at the whippings they had received. He broke into a run and the team followed his lead.

"Whoa! Whoa!" Hal cried out. He tripped and was pulled off his feet.

The dogs dashed on up the street as they scattered the remainder of the gear along the main street of Skagway.

The dogs and the scattered gear and clothes were rounded up.

"You need just half the load and twice the dogs, if you ever expect to reach Dawson," the men told Charles, Hal, and Mercedes.

Mercedes cried while she went through clothes, deciding what to keep. Although they went through every article until the load was cut in half, it was still too bulky.

Charles and Hal went out that evening and bought six "Outsider" dogs. This brought their team up to fourteen. But the newcomer dogs did not amount to much. They did not seem to know anything. Buck speedily taught them their places and what *not* to do, but he could not teach them what *to* do. They did not take kindly to trace and trail.

The two men were quite proud and cheerful as they set off down the trail with fourteen dogs—fourteen dogs not ready for the hard work ahead. Eight dogs were dead-tired and six dogs had never pulled a sled. But fourteen dogs they had! They had never seen a sled with so many as *fourteen dogs*!

In the Arctic, there was a reason why fourteen dogs should not drag one sled. This was that *one sled* could not carry the food needed for *fourteen dogs*. But Charles and Hal did not know this. They had worked the trip out with a pencil—so much to a dog, so many dogs, and so many days. It was all so *very* simple.

Buck felt that he could not depend upon these two men and the woman. They did not know how to do anything and did not want to learn.

They were lazy. It took them half the night to pitch camp, and half the morning to break that camp and get the sled loaded. Yet the work was so sloppy that for the rest of the day they had to stop to rearrange the load. Some days they did not make ten miles. On other days they were unable to get started at all. And all the while, the food supply was going down.

Chapter 10

HITTING THE BOTTOM

Of course they ran short on dog food.

Charles and Hal overfed the dogs at first. The six Outsider dogs had big appetites. Mercedes, with tears in her pretty eyes, could not get Charles to give the dogs more, so she stole from the fish sacks and fed them secretly. But it was not food that Buck and the huskies needed most—it was rest. And though they were making poor time, the heavy load they dragged took all their strength away.

Then the underfeeding began.

Hal realized one day that his dog food was half gone and they had covered very little distance.

They could not get more dog food, so he cut down on even the usual amount and tried to increase the day's travel. It was easy to give the dogs less food, but it was impossible to make the dogs travel faster. The men didn't know how to work dogs—they didn't even know how to work themselves.

The first to go was Dub. Poor thief that he was, always getting caught and punished, he had still been a faithful worker. The Outsider dogs did not last long. One by one they died.

By this time there was no joy in this Arctic adventure for any of the three people. Mercedes no longer wept over the dogs. She only wept over herself—except when she was quarreling with her husband and brother. And the three did quarrel. They were stiff and in pain. Their muscles ached, their bones ached, their very hearts ached. They had only hard words for each other. In the meantime, the fire remained unbuilt, the camp half-pitched, and the dogs unfed.

They thought only of their own misery and gave no thought to the animals. Through it all, Buck staggered along at the head of the starved team as if in a nightmare. He pulled when he could. When he could no longer pull, he fell down

and remained down till blows from whip or club drove him to his feet again. His once beautiful fur was dull and matted. He had become so thin that each rib and every bone in his body showed through his loose hide. It was heartbreaking—yet Buck's heart was unbreakable. The man in the red sweater had proved that many months before.

Buck's team of six dogs looked like skeletons. They no longer felt the pain of the whip, and their eyes looked lifeless. When the team stopped, they dropped down in the traces like dead dogs, with no spark left. When the club or whip fell upon them, the spark somehow fluttered, and they tottered to their feet and staggered on.

There came a day when Billee, the good-natured, fell and could not rise. Buck and the others knew their own time would be soon. On the next day Koona went, and only five of them remained. Joe was too ill to be mean. Pike was crippled and limping. Sol-leks, the one-eyed, was still faithful to his work—even in his agony. Teek, who had not traveled so far that winter, had been beaten more than the others. And Buck was still at the head of the team, but he was too weak to lead the starved, weary dogs.

The dogs were falling. Mercedes was weeping and riding. Hal and Charles were arguing. This was what they were doing when they staggered into John Thornton's camp at the mouth of the White River. When they stopped, the dogs dropped down as though they had all been struck dead. Mercedes dried her eyes and looked at John Thornton. Charles sat down on a log to rest. Hal did the talking. John Thornton was whittling an axe-handle. He whittled and listened, gave short replies and very little advice. He knew this type of traveler, and he knew they would not listen to advice.

John Thornton *did* tell them *not* to take chances on the ice. Hal waved his hand toward the frozen White River.

"They told us up in Skagway that we couldn't make White River, and here we are," said Hal with a jeer. "They said we should stay away from travel over ice, but we made it."

"And they told you true," John Thornton answered. "The ice is likely to bottom out at any moment. Only lucky fools could have made it. I tell you straight, I wouldn't risk my life on that ice for all the gold in Alaska."

"That's because you're not a fool, I suppose," said Hal. "All the same, we'll go on to Dawson." He took out his whip. "Get up there, Buck! Hi! Get up there! Mush on!"

Thornton went on whittling. He knew these fools would not listen.

But the team did not get up at the command and so the whip flashed out. John Thornton watched in silence. Sol-leks was the first to crawl to his feet. Teek followed. Joe came next, yelping with pain. Pike made painful efforts. Twice he fell over, when half-up, and on the third attempt managed to rise.

Buck made no effort. He lay quietly where he had fallen. The lash bit into him again and again. He did not whine or struggle. Several times Thornton started to speak, but changed his mind. Tears came to his eyes as the whipping went on.

This was the first time Buck had failed, and this angered Hal. No matter how he beat Buck, the poor dog would not budge. All day Buck had felt the thin, rotten ice under his feet. He sensed that danger lay ahead. He refused to stir. He felt numb. He no longer felt pain. He was slipping away.

*Buck was king—king over all the other dogs
and every person at the Miller estate.*

page 8

Day after day, Buck toiled in the traces.

page 47

*The visions of the hairy man
told him of the days of his ancestors.*
page 159

With a great cry from deep within him
he sings a song of the wild.
page 187

And then, suddenly, John Thornton sprang upon Hal. Mercedes screamed. Charles looked on in confusion. John Thornton stood over Buck, enraged.

"If you strike that dog again, I'll kill you," he said at last.

"It's my dog," Hal replied. "Get out of my way, or I'll fix you. I'm going to Dawson."

Thornton stood between him and Buck, and would not get out of the way. Hal drew his long hunting knife, but Thornton rapped Hal's knuckles with his axe handle, knocking the knife to the ground. Then he picked up the knife himself, and with two strokes cut Buck's traces.

Hal gave up on Buck—what use was he anymore, anyway? A few minutes later the Tenderfeet pulled out from the bank and out onto the frozen river. Buck heard them go and raised his head to see. Pike was leading, Sol-leks was at the wheel, and between were Joe and Teek. They were limping and staggering. Mercedes was riding the loaded sled. Hal guided at the gee-pole, and Charles stumbled along at the back.

As Buck watched them, Thornton knelt beside him and petted him with rough but kind hands. Dog and man both watched the sled crawling along over the ice. Suddenly, they saw its back end drop down and the gee-pole jerk into the air. Mercedes screamed. They saw Charles turn one step to run back. Then a whole section of ice gave way and dogs and humans disappeared.

THE CALL OF THE WILD

A white hole in the ice was all that was to be seen. The bottom had dropped out of the trail.

John Thornton and Buck looked at each other.

"You poor devil," said John Thornton and Buck licked his hand.

Chapter 11

FOR THE LOVE OF A MAN

When John Thornton's feet froze last
December, his partners made sure he was
comfortable before they left to get a raft in
Dawson. He was still limping slightly at the time
he rescued Buck. Together man and dog lay by
the riverbank through the long spring days,
watching the running water, listening to the
songs of birds and the hum of nature. John
Thornton improved and Buck slowly won back
his strength.

Buck could now be lazy as his wounds healed
and his muscles came back to cover his bones.
John Thornton's two dogs, Skeet and Night,

befriended Buck. Skeet was a little Irish setter who washed and cleansed Buck's wounds. Each morning after he had finished his breakfast, she attended to him. Night was a huge black dog, half-bloodhound and half-deerhound, with eyes that laughed with a good nature.

To Buck's surprise, these dogs showed no jealousy toward him. They seemed to share the kind nature of John Thornton. As Buck grew stronger they coaxed him into all sorts of ridiculous games, with John Thornton joining in. Buck romped through his time of healing and discovered a new feeling. Love. Real love for the first time. He had never really felt this before—not even for Judge Miller. But now, Buck came to love and adore John Thornton.

This man had saved his life. More than this, he was the ideal master. Other men had fed him and taken care of his needs, but John Thornton took care of his dogs as if they were his own children—because he truly cared. He never forgot to give a kind greeting or a cheering word. To sit down for a long talk with them was as much his delight as theirs.

He had a way of taking Buck's head roughly between his hands and, resting his own head upon Buck's, playfully shaking him back and forth. He growled names at him and cursed him lovingly. "You mean old rascal," Thornton would say. Buck found joy in this playful embrace, and, when the man released him, Buck sprang to his feet with his mouth and eyes laughing. John Thornton would exclaim, "Buck, you can all but speak!"

Buck expressed his love to this man in his own way. He would often seize Thornton's hand in his mouth and hold tight—biting hard enough to leave marks. Yet the man understood, wrestling the dog with spirit and joy.

Most of the time, however, Buck was content to adore from a distance. He went wild with happiness when Thornton touched him or spoke to him, but he did not seek this attention. Skeet liked to shove her nose under Thornton's hand and nudge and nudge till she was petted. Night would often walk up and rest his great head on Thornton's knee. But Buck was happy just to lie at Thornton's feet for hours, looking up into his face.

He studied the man's expressions and movements. And often, John Thornton would sense Buck's gaze and would turn to gaze back at the dog, without speech, his heart shining out of his eyes as Buck's heart shone out, too.

For a long time after his rescue, Buck did not want Thornton to be out of his sight. From the moment he left the tent to when he entered it again, Buck would follow at his heels. He was afraid that Thornton would pass out of his life as Perrault and François and the mail carriers had passed out. Even in the night, in his dreams, he was haunted by this fear. At such times he would creep through the chilly air to the flap of the tent, where he would stand and listen to the sound of his master's breathing.

But in spite of this great love for John Thornton, Buck's primitive nature remained strong within him. He was faithful and devoted to this man who had saved his life, but he could never be tamed again. The cruelty of other men and months on the trail had changed him forever. Deep inside, he was a thing of the wild, come in from the wild to sit by John Thornton's fire. Because of his very great love, he could not steal from this man, but from any *other* man, in any *other* camp, he did not hesitate to steal. His keen intelligence and primitive instincts were strong.

His face and body were marked by the teeth of many dogs, and he still fought as fiercely as ever.

Skeet and Night were too good-natured for quarreling—besides, they belonged to John Thornton. But any strange dog, no matter what the breed, swiftly gave in to Buck. He had learned well the law of club and fang, and he never showed mercy to any other dog. He had learned well from Spitz—show no weakness, fight to the end. The strongest dog who showed no fear would rule. Buck knew this all too well.

Deep in the forest, and deep within him, a call was sounding. Even as he lay by John Thornton's warm safe fire, he heard this call. Then he would turn his back upon the fire and plunge into the forest. He would run—on and on—though he knew not where or why. He did not wonder where or why, so strong was the call. But each time, the love for John Thornton drew him back to the fire again.

Thornton was the only man Buck could love. Sometimes travelers praised or petted Buck, but he would often get up and walk away. When Thornton's partners, Hans and Pete, arrived on the raft, Buck refused to notice them till he learned they were close friends with Thornton. Even then, along the entire raft trip up to Dawson, he mostly ignored these other men.

THE CALL OF THE WILD

For Thornton, however, his love seemed to grow and grow. He, alone among men, could put a pack upon Buck's back for the summer traveling. Nothing was too great for Buck to do when Thornton commanded.

"It's uncanny how Thornton and that dog seem to speak to each other," Pete noted one day.

"By Jingo, you are right," Hans answered. "Dat dog—him do anyt'ing for dat man. I hope no man ever get in the way between dem."

Chapter 12

THE SLED PULL

In Dawson that winter, Buck showed this uncanny loyalty and love for John Thornton.

The three partners had stopped off at a saloon one evening. "Black" Burton was there—an evil-tempered bully—and he was picking a fight with a young tenderfoot. Trying to hold tempers down, Thornton stepped in between. Buck, as was his custom, was lying in a corner of the room, head on paws, watching his master's every action. Black Burton struck out, without warning, and hit Thornton. He was sent spinning, and he saved himself from falling only by clutching the rail of the bar.

Those who were looking on heard something—not a bark nor a yelp—but something like a roar. They saw Buck's body rise up in the air as he left the floor for Burton's throat. The man saved his life by blocking with his arm, but was hurled backward with Buck on top of him. Then the crowd was upon Buck, and he was driven off.

While a doctor attended to Burton, Buck prowled up and down, growling, trying to rush in. Only heavy clubs could drive him back. A meeting was called on the spot, and all agreed that the dog had a just cause for attacking Burton. He was allowed to leave with Thornton, but his reputation was made. From that day, his name spread through every camp in Alaska.

Buck, because of his fame, was often compared to other dogs, and Thornton was driven to defend him. When the subject of dogs came up at the Eldorado Saloon one night, several men boasted of their favorites. At the end of half an hour, one man stated that *his* dog could start a sled with five hundred pounds and walk off with it. A second man bragged six hundred for *his* dog. A third, a man named Matthewson, boasted that *his* dog could start seven hundred.

"Hah!" said John Thornton. "Buck can start a thousand pounds."

"And break it out of the snow, and walk off with it for a hundred yards?" demanded Matthewson.

"And break it out, and walk off with it for a hundred yards," replied John Thornton.

"Well," Matthewson said slowly, so that all could hear, "I've got a thousand dollars that says he can't. And there it is." He slammed a sack of gold dust down upon the bar.

Nobody spoke. Thornton could feel a flush of warm blood creeping up his face. He did not know whether Buck could start a thousand pounds. Half a ton! He had great faith in Buck's strength, but how could he put Buck up to such a task? Plus, he didn't have a thousand dollars, and nor did Hans or Pete. The eyes of a dozen men fixed upon him, silent and waiting.

"I've got a sled standing outside right now with twenty fifty-pound sacks of flour on it," Matthewson went on. "We can put your dog to the test any time."

Thornton did not reply. He did not know what to say. He glanced from face to face, trying to gather his thoughts.

The face of Jim O'Brien, an old friend, caught Thornton's eyes. "Can you lend me a thousand?" he asked Jim, almost in a whisper.

"Sure," answered O'Brien, thumping down a sack next to Matthewson's. "Though I don't think, John, that the dog can do the trick."

The saloon emptied into the street. Several hundred men gathered to watch and bet on the outcome. Matthewson's sled, loaded with a thousand pounds of flour, had been standing for a couple of hours and the sled-runners had frozen fast to the hard-packed snow. Not a man believed the dog could even budge the sled, and they all bet against Buck.

Thornton looked at the sled itself, with the regular team of ten dogs still in harness. He had hurried into this foolishly and the task looked impossible. Matthewson, on the other hand, was quite pleased. "Three to one odds!" he proclaimed. "I'll bet you another thousand dollars, Thornton, what do you say?"

Thornton's doubt was strong, but so were his pride and his fighting spirit—the fighting spirit that does not care about the odds, that does not believe something is impossible.

Thornton went back into the saloon and called Hans and Pete to him. Together they came up with two hundred dollars. This was all they had, yet they laid it on the table.

The team of ten dogs was unhitched, and Buck was harnessed into the sled. He felt the excitement in the air, and he felt that in some way he must do a great thing for John Thornton. The men took note of this splendid animal. He was in perfect condition, with one hundred and fifty pounds of pure muscle and grit. His furry coat shone and every hair seemed to be alive. Men felt his muscles, proclaimed them hard as iron, and the odds went down to two to one.

"Gad, sir! Gad, sir!" stuttered one bearded man. "I offer you eight hundred dollars for him, sir, before the test. Eight hundred just as he stands."

Thornton shook his head and stepped over to Buck's side.

"You must stand off from him," Matthewson protested.

The crowd fell silent. Everybody saw that Buck was indeed a magnificent animal, but a thousand pounds—how could he break out and pull such a load?

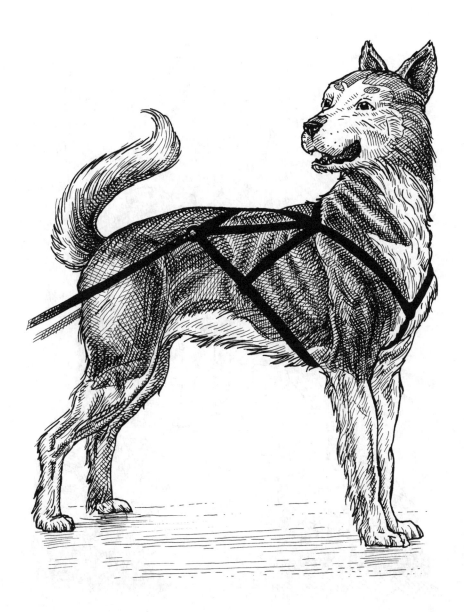

Thornton knelt down by Buck's side. He took his head in his hands and rested cheek on cheek. He did not playfully shake him, as he usually did, or tease him with words. Instead he just whispered in his ear, "As you love me, Buck. As you love me." Buck whined with an eagerness to please.

The crowd was watching curiously. This was odd—a man whispering to a dog. As Thornton got to his feet, Buck seized his mittened hand between his jaws, pressing in with his teeth and then letting go. It was the answer—not of speech, but of love. Thornton stepped well back.

"Now, Buck," he said.

Buck tightened the traces, then let them loosen a bit. It was the way he had learned.

"*Gee!*" Thornton's voice rang out sharply.

Buck swung to the right with all his might. The load quivered, and from under the runners arose a crisp crackling.

"*Haw!*" Thornton commanded.

Buck pulled this time to the left. The crackling turned into a snapping. The runners slipped several inches to the side. The sled was broken out! Every man was holding his breath.

JACK LONDON

THE CALL OF THE WILD

"Now, *MUSH!*"

Thornton's command cracked out like a pistol shot. Buck threw himself forward. His whole body—and every muscle—went into the effort. His great chest was low to the ground, his head forward and down, while his feet were flying like mad, the claws digging into the hard-packed snow. The sled swayed slightly. One of Buck's feet slipped, and one man groaned aloud. The sled jerked ahead… half an inch… an inch… two inches… The jerks became fewer until the sled was moving ahead slowly, slowly, steadily…

Men gasped and began to breathe again. Thornton was running behind, encouraging Buck with short, cheery words. As he neared the pile of firewood that marked the end of the hundred yards, a cheer began to grow and grow, which burst into a roar as he passed the firewood and halted at command. Every man began to jump with joy and wonder—even Matthewson. Hats and mittens were flying in the air. Men were shaking hands and bubbling over in a general excitement.

But Thornton fell on his knees beside Buck. Head was against head, and he was shaking him back and forth. Those close by heard him roughing

it up and growling words at Buck, softly and lovingly. "You old rascal. You darned old rascal!"

"I'll give you a thousand dollars for him, sir, a thousand, sir!" exclaimed the bearded man.

Thornton rose to his feet. His eyes were wet. The tears were streaming down his cheeks. "Sir," he said, "no, sir. You can forget it, sir."

Buck seized Thornton's hand in his teeth. Thornton shook him back and forth. Man and dog romped, alone within their special love for each other, while all the men looked on in wonder.

Chapter 13

THE SOUNDING OF THE CALL

Sixteen hundred dollars! Buck earned John Thornton enough money to travel with his partners into the East in search of a "lost" gold mine. Many men had looked for it. Few had found it. And many had never returned from their search. Yet there were stories that told of this lost mine near an old cabin—a mine with the most fantastic gold nuggets.

John Thornton, Pete, and Hans, with Buck and six other dogs, went in search of this old cabin and this treasure. John Thornton was not afraid of the wild. He was at home on any trail. He hunted for food and traveled light.

To Buck it was a great life, this hunting, fishing, and wandering through strange places. The months came and went. They faced blizzards and bitter cold in the winter months and gnats and flies in the warm months. They rafted across blue mountain lakes, and drifted down rivers in slender boats carved from tree trunks. Sometimes they went hungry, sometimes they feasted. This was adventure!

And through another winter they wandered. Then spring came on once more, and at the end of all their wandering they found not the "lost mine and old cabin," but a shallow placer—a deposit of gravel where gold is often found. Here the gold showed like yellow butter across the bottom of the washing pan!

Each day they worked they earned thousands of dollars in clean dust and nuggets, and they worked every day. The gold was sacked in moose-hide bags, fifty pounds to the bag. With no more thought of the "lost mine," they heaped their treasure up.

There was very little for the dogs to do, and Buck spent long hours by the fire. The vision of the short-legged hairy man came to him more often.

Buck gazed into the fire and could see the hairy man—as if in a dream—living with fear in that other world.

He watched the hairy man sleeping by the fire, crouched with his hands over his head in fear. Sometimes Buck dreamed that they walked on a beach, gathering shellfish. Even then, the hairy man was alert to hidden danger, ready to run like the wind.

Buck felt the wild stirrings of his own soul. The visions of the hairy man told him of the days of his ancestors. But the sounds and calls from the forest told him of a new life waiting now. Sometimes he followed the call into the forest, looking for it, barking softly. He would thrust his nose into the earth and moss. He would crouch for hours, wide-eyed and wide-eared to all that moved and sounded about him.

When the call came to him, he listened. He would be dozing lazily in camp when suddenly his head would lift and his ears cock up, listening. He would spring to his feet and dash away, on and on, for hours, through the forest and across the open spaces. For a day at a time he would lie in the underbrush where he could watch the birds and wildlife. But especially he loved to run at midnight, listening to the sleepy murmurs of the forest, and seeking the mysterious "something" that called—called, waking or sleeping, at all times, for him to come.

One night he sprang from sleep with a start, with a scent in his nostrils. From the forest came the call—a long howl. And he knew it, in the old familiar way, as a sound he had heard before. He sprang through the sleeping camp and dashed through the woods.

As he drew closer to the cry he went more slowly, with caution in every movement, till he came to an open place among the trees. Looking out he saw a long, lean timber wolf with his nose pointed to the sky.

Buck had made no noise, yet the wolf stopped howling. Buck stalked into the open, half-crouching, with his tail straight and stiff. He was ready for either an attack or surrender. But the wolf fled at the sight of him. Buck followed, with wild leapings. He ran the wolf into a jammed creek bed, cornering him. The wolf whirled about, snarling and clipping his teeth together.

Buck did not attack, but circled about him in a friendly manner. The wolf was suspicious and afraid. Seeing his chance, the wolf darted away, and the chase was on again. Time and again he was cornered, and then the wolf would escape.

But in the end, the wolf surrendered to Buck's chase and finally sniffed noses with him. Then they became friendly, and romped about like brothers. After some time of this, the wolf started off in a way that plainly showed he was going somewhere. He made it clear to Buck that he was to come. They ran side by side through the early morning hours, straight up the creek bed, and up onto the mountainside.

They came down into a large forest with many streams, and through this wild area they ran on, hour after hour. The sun rose higher and the day grew warmer. Buck was wildly glad. He knew he was at last answering the call, running by the side of his wood brother toward the place where the call came from. Instincts and old memories were stirring within him. He had done this thing before, somewhere in that other world—his dream world. And he was doing it again now, running free in the open with the wide sky overhead.

THE CALL OF THE WILD

They stopped by a running stream to drink. Then Buck remembered John Thornton. He sat down. The wolf started on toward the place from where the call surely came, then returned to Buck, sniffing noses. But Buck turned about and started slowly back to camp.

For an hour the wild brother ran by his side, whining softly. Then he sat down, pointed his nose upward, and howled. It was a sad howl, and as Buck trotted back to camp he heard it grow faint and then fainter until it was lost in the distance.

John Thornton was eating dinner when Buck dashed into camp and sprang upon him in a playful romp, licking his face, biting his hand. John Thornton shook Buck back and forth and growled and spoke to him lovingly.

For two days and nights, Buck never left camp and never let Thornton out of his sight. He followed him about at his work, watched him while he ate, saw him into his blankets at night and out of them in the morning. But after two days the call in the forest began to sound more than ever.

Buck thought of his wild brother and of the smiling, wild land that lay outside camp. Once again he took to wandering in the woods, but the wild brother came no more. Buck listened every night. The sad howl was never raised.

Chapter 14

INTO THE WILDS

Buck began to sleep out at night, staying away from camp for days at a time. Once he crossed the mountain and went down into the land of timber and streams. There he wandered for a week, looking for his wild brother. He fished for salmon and hunted for his food. He killed only to eat. And he was quick, smart, and crafty. No prey was too swift for him—bird, rabbit, or beaver.

By the stream he killed a large black bear that was blinded by the mosquitoes. The bear had raged through the forest with Buck at his heels. It was a hard fight, but Buck took the bear down. He was a master in the wild.

Buck could rely on his own strength and power. His pride showed in the way he carried himself, in every muscle. He looked like a gigantic wolf and he was cunning like a wolf. Yet he had the intelligence of his shepherd mother and St. Bernard father. All this made him one of the fiercest creatures to roam the wild. Every part of him was aware of the sounds and smells and sights around him. He could think faster than any dog and hunt as well as any wild wolf. Even the men noticed that Buck was special.

"Never was there such a dog," said John Thornton one day, as they watched Buck march out of camp.

"When he was made, the mold was broke," said Pete.

"I t'ink so myself," Hans affirmed.

They saw Buck marching out of camp, but they did not see the instant and terrible change that took place as soon as he was within the forest. There he became a thing of the wild, stealing along softly, cat-footed, like a passing shadow.

As the fall of the year came on, the moose herds began to appear. Buck came upon a band of twenty moose one day at the creek. Their chief

was a great bull moose, standing over six feet from the ground. Buck watched the bull moose. Here was a challenge. Back and forth the bull tossed his great antlers. His small eyes glared as he roared with fury at the sight of Buck.

A feathered arrow was sticking out of the bull's side. He was wounded, and Buck took note of this. Buck followed the bull moose and cut him off from the others. Buck barked and danced about in front of the bull, just out of reach of the great antlers and terrible hoofs. The bull was driven into a rage. He charged at Buck, but the crafty dog backed away, toying with the great animal.

Buck was patient. For half a day he kept at the wounded bull. He attacked from all sides, keeping the moose from rejoining the others. The herd tried to help their leader from time to time, but they soon tired of the fierce dog.

As night came, the weary old bull stood with his head lowered. He watched the other moose as they went off in search of food. He could not follow. The fanged dog would not let him go. He was a grand animal and had lived a long, strong life. At the end he faced death at the teeth of another grand animal—a new king.

From then on, night and day, Buck never left the moose. He would not let him eat. He would not let him drink. Buck kept at him, nipping at his legs, waiting for the great bull moose to grow weaker and weaker. At last, at the end of the fourth day, he pulled the great moose down.

For a day and a night he remained by the kill, eating and sleeping. Then he turned his face toward camp and John Thornton.

As he set out on the path for home, he could feel a new stir in the land. He knew—not by sight, or sound, or smell, but by some other sense—that new life was coming into the land. The birds talked of it, the squirrels chattered about it, the very breeze whispered of it. Several times he stopped and drew in the fresh morning air in great sniffs. He read a message which made him leap on with greater speed. He now felt a sense of dread, and as he dropped down into the valley toward camp, he proceeded with greater caution.

Three miles away he came upon a fresh trail that sent his neck hair bristling. It led straight toward camp and John Thornton. Buck hurried on swiftly, with every nerve tense, alert to the details which told a story—all but the end.

He noticed the silence of the forest, as if all life was in hiding.

As Buck slid along like a shadow, his nose picked up a scent that pulled him toward a thicket. There he found Night. He was lying on his side, dead, with a feathered arrow through his body.

From the camp came the faint sound of many voices, rising and falling in a sing-song chant. Bellying forward to the edge of the clearing, he found Hans, lying on his face, feathered with arrows. Then Buck peered out through the trees and saw what made his hair leap straight up on his neck and shoulders. Rage swept over him. He did not know that he growled so loudly. His reason left him and his great love for John Thornton made him react without thinking.

The Yeehats were dancing about the camp's fire when they heard a fearful roaring and saw rushing upon them an animal—a strange and fierce animal they had never seen before. It was Buck, a live hurricane of fury, hurling himself upon them in a frenzy to destroy. He sprang at the closest man, the chief of the Yeehats, grabbing his throat. He did not pause, but leaped

JACK LONDON

THE CALL OF THE WILD

upon a second man. He plunged so quickly that every arrow missed him. In fact, the surprised Indians were so close together and so frantic that they shot one another with the arrows. Then a panic seized the Yeehats, and they fled in terror to the woods, yelling as they fled that the Evil Spirit had come.

And truly Buck was the Evil Spirit raging at their heels and dragging them down like deer as they raced through the trees. It was a fateful day for the Yeehats. They scattered—and it was not till a week later that the last of the survivors gathered together in a lower valley and counted their losses.

Buck, weary of the chase, returned to the empty camp. He found Pete dead in his blankets. Thornton's own struggle was fresh-written on the earth and Buck scented every detail of it down to the edge of a deep pool. By the water's edge lay Skeet, faithful to the end. The pool was muddy and Buck could not see what it contained. But he knew that it contained John Thornton, for Buck followed his trace into the water.

No trace led away.

All day Buck brooded by the pool or roamed about the camp. Buck knew death, and he knew John Thornton was dead. It left him empty. He ached and ached and nothing could fill this emptiness. At times, when he paused at the bodies of the Yeehats, he forgot his pain. He was aware of a great pride in himself. He had killed man and he had killed in the face of the law of club and fang. Never again would he fear this animal.

Chapter 15

BUCK ANSWERS THE CALL

Night came on, and a full moon rose high over the trees into the sky. Buck, lying next to the pool, lifted his head from his mourning and brooding. He stood up, listening and scenting. From far away drifted a faint, sharp yelp, followed by more sharp yelps. He walked to the center of the open space and listened. It was the call—the call of the wild. And now he was ready to follow. John Thornton was dead. The last tie with man was broken.

A wolf pack had crossed over from the land of streams and timber and invaded Buck's valley. Into the clearing they poured, lit by the moonlight.

In the center of the clearing stood Buck, as still as a statue, waiting for them.

They stopped in wonder at this large creature before them. The boldest one leaped straight for him. Like a flash, Buck struck, breaking the neck. Three others tried it, and one after the other they drew back, cut and slashed.

The whole pack then closed in. Buck was too quick and too smart for them. Whirling on his hind legs, and snapping and gashing, he was everywhere at once, leaping from side to side. To prevent the pack from getting behind him, he was forced back down into the creek bed. Here he was finally backed against a high gravel bank. He turned and faced the pack.

For half an hour no wolf could take the cornered beast and the wolves drew back. They remained there. Some were lying down, others were on their feet, watching him. Still others were lapping water from the pool.

One wolf, long and lean and gray, came to Buck slowly, in a friendly manner. Buck recognized his wild brother with whom he had run for a night and a day. He was whining softly, and, as Buck whined, they touched noses.

Then an old battle-scarred wolf came forward. Buck snarled his lips, but sniffed noses with him. The old wolf sat down, pointed nose at the moon, and broke out the long wolf howl. The others sat down and howled. And now the call came to Buck. He, too, sat down and howled.

The pack crowded around him, sniffing. The leaders lifted the call of the pack and sprang away into the woods. The wolves swung in behind, yelping in chorus. And Buck ran with them, side by side with the wild brother, yelping as he ran.

And here may well end the story of Buck.

But it was not many years before the Yeehats noted a change in the breed of timber wolves. Some had splashes of brown on head and muzzle, and a strip of white down the chest. But more remarkable than this, the Yeehats tell of a Ghost Dog that runs at the head of the pack. They are afraid of this Ghost Dog, for it has great cunning—stealing from their camps, robbing their traps, and killing their dogs.

Nay, the tale grows worse. The Indians tell of hunters who never returned to the camp. And they tell of hunters found dead—with wolf prints about them in the snow. These prints were far greater than the prints of any wolf. Each fall, when the Yeehats follow the moose herds, there is a certain valley they never enter. There are women who become sad when the tale is told around the fire of how the Evil Spirit came to live in that valley.

In the summers there is one visitor to that valley, however, that the Yeehats never see. It is a great, beautiful wolf unlike all other wolves. He comes alone from the timber land and walks down into an open space among the trees. Here a golden stream flows into a still pond. He stays by the pond for a time, howling once, long and mournfully, before he departs.

But he is not always alone. When the long winter nights come on, he may be seen running at the head of the pack through the pale moonlight. With a great cry from deep within him he sings a song of the wild, which is the song of the pack.

THE END

WHITE FANG

CONTENTS

CONTENTS

CHARACTERS

BILL AND HENRY: two dogsledders

FATTY, FROG, SPANKER, ONE EAR: dogs on Bill and Henry's team

SHE-WOLF: White Fang's mother, who is half dog, called Kiche by the Indians

ONE EYE: a wolf, White Fang's father, who is blind in one eye

WHITE FANG: (The Fighting Wolf, Wolf) the gray cub, who survives the trials of the Wild and life at the hands of man-animals

MOTHER LYNX: gives the she-wolf and the gray cub a tough fight

GRAY BEAVER, KLOO-KOOCH, MIT-SAH: the Indian man and his family, who own Kiche and White Fang

LIP-LIP: a bully among the Indian dogs and White Fang's rival

BASEEK: the first full-grown dog White Fang faces down

CHARACTERS

BEAUTY SMITH: White Fang's second owner, a cruel coward who enjoys seeing dogs fight

TIM KEENAN: the owner of the bulldog, Cherokee, that fights White Fang

WEEDON SCOTT: the master who truly cares for White Fang

MATT: a dog-musher who helps Weedon teach White Fang

JUDGE SCOTT: Weedon's father, who cannot quite trust a wolf

MRS. SCOTT, BETH, AND MARY: Weedon's mother and sisters

ALICE: Weedon's wife

WEEDON AND MAUD: Weedon's children

Chapter 1

THE SHE-WOLF

Down the frozen waterway pawed a string of wolfish dogs. Ice clung to their fur, and their breath froze in the air. Leather harnesses were on the dogs, and leather traces attached them to a sled which dragged along behind. On the sled, securely tied, was a long and narrow box.

One man worked ahead of the dogs, on wide snowshoes. Another man worked at the back of the sled. Their bodies were covered with fur and soft leather. Their eyelashes and cheeks and lips were coated with ice from their frozen breath. On the sled, in the box, lay a third man whose work was over—a dead man.

They traveled without talking. On every side was silence. An hour went by, and a second hour. The pale light of the sunless day was beginning to fade. A faint, far cry arose on the still air. Then another. The front man turned his head until his eyes met the eyes of the man behind.

"They're after us, Bill," said the front man.

"Meat is scarce," answered his friend. "I ain't seen rabbit tracks for days."

After this, they spoke no more.

When it got dark they made camp. The wolf-dogs gathered on the far side of the fire.

"Henry," asked Bill, munching on beans, "how many dogs have we got?"

"Six."

"Well, Henry... We've got six dogs. I took six fish out of the bag. I gave one fish to each dog an', Henry, I was one fish short. I had to go back to the bag to get One Ear a fish."

"We've only got six dogs," Henry said.

"I won't say they was all dogs," Bill went on, "but there was seven of 'em that got fish. I saw the other one run off across the snow."

"I'll be almighty glad when this trip's over."

"What d'ye mean by that?" Bill demanded.

"I mean that you're beginnin' to see things."

"The tracks is there in the snow," Bill answered. "I'll show 'em to you."

"Then you're thinkin' it was—" A long wailing cry from somewhere in the darkness interrupted him. "—one of *them*?"

Bill nodded.

From every side the cries arose and grew louder. The dogs huddled closer to the fire.

"Henry, I was a-thinking…" said Bill. "That man there in the box is a sight luckier than we'll ever be. Long distance funerals is something you an' me can't afford. Why a man as rich as him wanted to come up here is more than I can see."

Bill started to speak, but then pointed out toward the wall of darkness. There they saw a pair of eyes gleaming like red coals. Then a second pair. Then a third. The sled dogs became afraid and rushed over to the men.

"Henry, it's real unlucky that we're out of rifle cartridges."

Henry stopped spreading blankets. "How many cartridges did you say you had left?"

"Three. And I wish it was three hundred!" Bill shook his fist at the gleaming eyes.

WHITE FANG

The men crawled into bed and slept, side by side, under one covering. The fire died down, and the gleaming eyes drew closer. The dogs huddled in fear. Once the dogs' cries became so loud that Bill woke up. He got out of bed and threw more wood on the fire. As it began to flame up, the circle of eyes drew farther back. He glanced at the huddled dogs and rubbed his eyes.

"Henry," he said.

Henry groaned, "What's wrong now?"

"There's seven of 'em again."

Not really hearing, Henry grunted and drifted back to sleep.

In the darkness of the morning, Henry made breakfast, while Bill made the sled ready.

"Say, Henry," Bill called, "one of the dogs is gone! Now there's only five."

Henry rushed over and counted the dogs. "You're right. Fatty's gone. Just like that? They couldn't jes' swallow him alive…"

"We didn't hear nothin'," Bill added.

"Surely he didn't run off. Not out there. Not to them. What would make a dog follow after them? That would be killing his fool self."

"But Fatty's gone, sure as the world."

WHITE FANG

The men launched into the darkness. They heard the wolves howling all day long.

That night, Henry was adding ice to cool the bubbling pot of beans. He was suddenly startled by a shout from Bill and a snarling cry of pain from among the dogs. Looking, he saw Bill amid the dogs. In one hand he held a stout club, in the other the chewed tail of a sun-cured salmon.

"It got half of it," he announced, "but I got a whack in just the same."

"What'd it look like?" Henry asked.

"Like any dog."

"Must be a tame wolf."

———

The next morning, Bill shouted, "Frog's gone."

Henry counted the dogs, and then joined his partner in cursing the wolves that had robbed them of another dog.

"Frog was the strongest of the bunch," Bill said.

They ate a gloomy breakfast. Then they harnessed the four remaining dogs to the sled. The day was the same as the others before—all work and silence, except for the wailing wolves.

That night, Bill not only tied up the dogs, but he also tied them so they couldn't chew themselves free.

"If we could put a couple of shot into 'em," Henry remarked, "those wolves would be more respectful."

A sound among the dogs attracted the men's attention. Full into the firelight glided a doglike animal. It moved slowly, watching the men, then fixing its eyes on the dogs.

"That fool One Ear don't seem scairt much," Bill said in a low tone.

"It's a she-wolf," Henry whispered back. "She's the decoy for the pack. She draws out the dog. Then the other wolves pitches in an' eats him up."

The fire crackled. A log fell apart with a loud spluttering noise. At the sound, the strange animal leaped back into the darkness.

"Henry, I'm a-thinkin'," Bill said, "that was the one I whopped with the club."

"It knows for certain more than a self-respectin' wolf ought to know," Henry agreed. "A wolf that knows enough to come in with the dogs at feedin' time has been around people."

"Part dog, for sure," said Bill.

WHITE FANG

In the morning, Henry renewed the fire and cooked breakfast.

As soon as Bill sat down to eat, Henry said, "Spanker's gone."

Bill counted the dogs. "How'd it happen?"

Henry shrugged his shoulders. "Don't know. One Ear must have chewed Spanker loose."

"I'll tie 'em up out of reach of each other tonight," Bill said.

They took to the trail, anxious to reach the town of McGurry—and to be rid of the hungry wolves that followed just out of sight.

As the cold gray of the afternoon came on, Bill slipped the rifle from under the sled lashings.

"You keep right on, Henry," he said. "I'm goin' to see what I can see."

"You'd better stick by the sled," his partner replied. "You've only got three cartridges."

Bill didn't listen. He disappeared into the gray quiet. An hour later, he came back to the sled.

"The wolves are scattered wide, lookin' for other game and followin' us. They're thin. They ain't had nothin' to eat in weeks, I reckon, except our dogs. There's so many wolves, *that* didn't feed 'em much."

A few minutes later, Henry, who was now behind the sled, gave a low, warning whistle. Bill turned and stopped the dogs.

"It's the she-wolf," Bill whispered.

Just behind them on the trail trotted a furry, slinking wolf. The animal came forward a few steps. It repeated this several times, till it was a short hundred yards away.

"Biggest wolf I ever seen," Henry commented.

"Kind of a strange red color," Bill answered, "like a husky. Hey, hey, come here, you husky!"

"Ain't a bit scairt of you," Henry laughed.

Bill waved his hand and shouted, but the animal showed no fear. The men were meat and the wolf was hungry.

"We've got three cartridges," Bill said. "It's a dead shot. She's killed three already. The dogs will want to follow her 'cause she's part dog. What do you say I shoot it?"

Henry nodded. But before Bill could get the rifle to his shoulder, the she-wolf leaped into a clump of spruce trees and disappeared.

"I might have knowed it," Bill said. "A wolf that knows enough to come in with the dogs at feedin' time would know all about guns."

WHITE FANG

They camped early that night. Before they went to bed, Bill saw to it that the dogs were tied out of gnawing-reach of one another.

But the wolves were growing bolder.

"They're goin' to get us," Bill remarked as he listened to the growls and the fire-crackle.

"They've half got you already, a-talkin' like that," Henry retorted sharply. "A man's half-licked when he says he is. And you're half-eaten from the way you're goin' on."

Chapter 2

THE HUNGER CRY

The day began well enough. They had lost no dogs during the night. They swung upon the trail and darkness with lighter spirits. Bill even made a few jokes when the sled accidentally overturned.

With the sled upside down, they had to unharness the dogs to straighten out the tangle. Henry saw One Ear creeping away.

"Here, you, One Ear!" he cried.

But One Ear broke into a run. And there, out in the snow, was the she-wolf waiting for him. She moved toward him a few steps, playfully, and then halted. Every step forward that he took, she took one back.

Too late, One Ear learned his mistake. A dozen wolves bounded across the snow. The she-wolf snarled and sprang. One Ear thrust her off and tried to circle back toward the sled.

"Where are you goin'?" Henry demanded, laying his arm on Bill's arm.

"I won't stand it," Bill said. "They ain't a-goin' to get any more of our dogs." Gun in hand, he plunged into the underbrush.

"Don't take no chances!" Henry called after him. He sat down on the sled and watched.

All too quickly, Henry heard three shots and he knew that Bill's ammunition was gone. One Ear yelped. A wolf cried out. And that was all. Silence.

Henry sat for a long while upon the sled. No need to get up. He knew what had happened. The two dogs crouched and trembled at his feet.

At last, he passed a rope over his shoulder and pulled the sled along the trail with the dogs. At the first hint of darkness he made camp.

But he could not sleep that night. Before his eyes closed, the wolves had drawn too near for safety. Henry kept the fire blazing. It was the only thing that kept him from their hungry fangs. His two dogs stayed close to him, one on each side.

In the morning, the man was tired and wide-eyed from lack of sleep. He cooked breakfast in the darkness. After daylight, the wolves moved back. Then Henry chopped down saplings and built a deck high up between two trees. Using sled lashings, he hoisted the coffin up on top.

"They got Bill, an' they may get me, but they'll never get you," he said to the dead body.

Then he started off. The wolves were now following in the open. They trotted lazily behind, their red tongues hanging out.

At midday, Henry stopped and chopped a large supply of firewood.

With night came horror. The starving wolves were growing bolder. And Henry was suffering from lack of sleep. He dozed, crouching by the fire, wrapped in blankets. The axe lay between his knees, and the dogs stayed close against him.

Once, he came out of a doze to see the red-colored she-wolf not more than six feet away. She took no notice of the two dogs. She was looking at the man. She licked her chops.

He reached for a burning stick. But even as he reached, she sprang back. He knew that she was used to having things thrown at her.

All night, with burning sticks, he fought off the hungry pack. Morning came, but for the first time the wolves stayed in a circle about him in the light of day. The moment he left the protection of the fire, the boldest wolf leaped for him—but leaped short and sprang back, snapping his jaws.

The rest of the pack was now up. The man threw fiery sticks right and left to drive them back to a safe distance. Even in the daylight he did not dare leave the fire to chop fresh wood.

The night was the same as the night before, except that the man was even sleepier. Even the snarling of the dogs could not keep him awake. Once, after drifting off, he awoke with a start. The she-wolf was less than a yard from him. He thrust a burning stick into her snarling mouth. She sprang away, yelling with pain.

Before long, the man's eyes closed again. He dreamed. He dreamed he was safe inside Fort McGurry. It was warm and comfortable. Then, suddenly, wolves were howling at the fort gates. And then, in his dream, there was a crash. The door burst open. Wolves filled the room, leaping straight for him. And the howling—the loud howling—it was so clear—

And then he awoke to find the howling real. The wolves were rushing in—and were upon him! Without thinking, he leaped into the fire. Then began a firefight. His mittens protected his hands, and he scooped live coals into the air in every direction. The campfire looked like a volcano.

His face was blistering. His eyebrows and lashes were singed off. The heat was burning through his moccasins. With a flaming stick in each hand, he sprang to the edge of the fire. His two dogs were missing, and he well knew that they had been taken.

"You ain't got me yet!" he cried, shaking a fist at the snarling pack.

He set to work on a new idea. He pulled the fire out into a large circle, and crouched within the

circle of coals. The pack came curiously to the rim of the fire to see what had become of him. Then the she-wolf sat down, pointed her nose to a star, and began to howl. One by one the wolves joined her in the hunger cry.

Dawn came, and daylight. The fire was burning low. The fuel had run out. The man sat down. His shoulders drooped and his head fell to his knees. He had given up the struggle.

"I guess you can come an' get me any time," he mumbled. "Anyway, I'm goin' to sleep."

Once he awakened and he saw the she-wolf gazing at him.

Again he awakened, a little later, though it seemed hours to him. A mysterious change had taken place. The wolves were gone!

There were cries of men, and four sleds pulled in. Half a dozen men rushed to the man crouched inside the dying circle of fire.

"Red she-wolf…" he mumbled. "First she ate the dog food… Then she ate the dogs… An' after that she ate Bill…"

"Where's Lord Alfred?" one man yelled.

Bill shook his head. "No, she didn't eat him… He's roostin' in a tree in his box. Say, you lemme alone. I'm too tired. Goo'night, everybody."

His eyes fluttered and went shut. The men eased him down upon the blankets as his snores rose on the frosty air.

But there was another sound, far and faint in the distance. It was the cry of the hungry wolf pack as it took to the trail of other meat.

——————— *Chapter 3* ———————

THE BATTLE OF THE FANGS

It was the she-wolf who first heard the sounds of men's voices. And it was the she-wolf who was first to spring away from Henry and run into the darkness at the sound of his rescue.

Leading the pack was a large gray wolf. The she-wolf ran beside him. On her other side ran a thin old wolf, grizzled and marked with battle scars. He ran always on her right side, for his left eye was blind. At the back limped the weak members, the very young and the very old. At the front were the strongest.

Tired and starving, they ran on—day and night—over a frozen, dead world. No life stirred.

Finally, they came upon a bull moose. Here was meat and life, with no fires to guard it. The struggle was fierce, but the moose was brought down, and there was food in plenty. The wolves ate their fill. There was now resting and sleeping. The famine was over. The wolves were now in the world of life and game.

There came a day when the wolf pack split. The she-wolf, the young leader on her left, and the one-eyed elder on her right, led half the pack to the east. Each day, wolves left this group, until only four were left—the she-wolf, the young leader, the one-eyed one, and an eager three-year-old male.

The three-year-old grew daring. He attacked the one-eyed elder on his blind side. The third wolf joined the elder. Together, they attacked the three-year-old. Forgotten were the days when they had hunted together, and the hunger they had suffered. The time for mating was at hand.

The she-wolf, the cause of it all, sat down and watched as the two older wolves killed the three-year-old. But it was not over. When the young leader stopped to lick his wounds, the old one-eyed leader saw his chance. He leaped and his teeth tore at the younger leader's throat.

Bleeding and coughing, the young leader sprang at the elder and fought while life faded from him. Finally, the young leader lay in the snow and moved no more.

The days passed by, and One Eye and the she-wolf kept together, alone, hunting, killing, and eating their meat together. They did not remain in one place, but traveled across country until they came to the Mackenzie River.

There, one moonlit night, One Eye suddenly halted. The she-wolf trotted on, unalarmed. To their ears came the sounds of dogs scuffling, the rough cries of men, the voices of scolding women, and once the high cry of a child. And to their nostrils came the many smells of an Indian camp. One Eye did not know these sounds and these smells. But the she-wolf knew them well.

Old One Eye started slowly to go. The she-wolf turned and touched his neck with her muzzle. She wanted them to join the Indian camp. She felt an urge to go forward, to be in closer to that fire, to be squabbling with the dogs, and dodging the stumbling feet of men.

Eventually, One Eye was able to make her follow him—away from the camp.

WHITE FANG

As they traveled, they came upon a fresh rabbit trail. Both noses went down. One Eye caught sight of a white form on the white snow. He raced ahead after the fleeing animal. Leap by leap he gained. One leap more and it would be his. But that leap was never made. High in the air—and straight up—soared the white form. The snowshoe rabbit danced above him, struggling in the air, never to return to the ground.

One Eye sprang back with a snort of sudden fright. He crouched in the snow and snarled up at this thing he did not understand. But the she-wolf thrust coolly past him. She sprang for the dancing rabbit, but missed. She made another failed leap, and another.

One Eye watched her. He now made a mighty spring upward himself. His teeth closed upon the rabbit, and he pulled it back to earth. But at the same time there was a crackling movement beside him. A young spruce sapling was bending down above him to strike him! His jaws let go of the rabbit, and he leaped backward to escape this strange danger. The sapling snapped upright— and the rabbit soared into the air again.

WHITE FANG

The she-wolf was angry. She lunged at One Eye, then sat down in the snow. Old One Eye was now more afraid of his mate than the mysterious bending sapling. He again sprang for the rabbit. As he sank back with it between his teeth, he kept his eye on the sapling. As before, it followed him to earth. He crouched, waiting for the blow. But the blow did not come. The sapling remained bent above him.

The she-wolf took the rabbit from him, and while the sapling swayed above her she calmly gnawed the rabbit loose. At once the sapling shot up—and after that gave no more trouble. One Eye and the she-wolf ate the rabbit body that the strange sapling had caught for them.

There were other trails where rabbits were hanging in the air. Following the she-wolf's wise ways, One Eye soon learned the method of robbing snares. This was to serve him well in the days to come.

Chapter 4

FIVE CUBS TO FEED

For two days the she-wolf and One Eye hung about the Indian camp. One morning, the air popped with the sound of a rifle, and a bullet smashed against a tree several inches from One Eye's head. They left the camp, but did not go far.

The she-wolf was trotting wearily along a small, rocky, frozen stream when she came upon a high, overhanging bank. The spring storms and melting snows had worn out an area in the bank. In one place, this had made a small cave.

She paused at the mouth of the cave. She looked the wall over carefully. It was dry and cozy. She finally entered its narrow mouth.

One Eye was hungry. He lay down in the entrance and slept, but did not sleep well. He tried to persuade his mate to get up, but she only snarled at him. So he walked out alone into the bright sunshine. He went up the frozen bed of the stream. He was gone for hours, and he came back through the darkness hungrier than when he had started. He had found game, but had not caught it.

He paused at the mouth of the cave. Faint, strange sounds came from within. He crawled inside on his belly and was met by a warning snarl from the she-wolf. He curled up and slept in the entrance.

When morning light came, One Eye could see, snuggled against her body, five strange little bundles of life. He went back outside to hunt.

Five or six miles from the cave, the stream divided into two forks. One Eye took the left fork going off between the mountains, and came upon a fresh track. The footprint was large—larger than his. He turned back and took the right fork. Within half a mile, his quick ears caught the sound of a porcupine gnawing on a tree. One Eye approached carefully.

The porcupine rolled itself into a ball. In his youth, One Eye had sniffed too near a ball of quills such as this—and the tail had flicked out suddenly in his face. So he lay down, his nose a foot away. After a while, he arose and trotted on. In the afternoon he came upon a grouse. The bird made a startled rise, but One Eye struck it with his paw, and caught it as it fluttered across the snow.

He headed for the cave with the grouse in his mouth. Near the stream, he came upon more of the large tracks he had seen that morning. He slid his head around a corner of rock. There he saw the maker of the tracks—a large female lynx. She was crouching in front of the tight-rolled ball of quills. One Eye lay hidden in the snow.

Half an hour passed—an hour—and nothing happened. At last, the porcupine decided that its enemy had gone. In the instant it began to unroll, the lynx struck. Everything happened at once—the blow, the tail flick, the squeal from the porcupine, the big cat's squall when it was stuck full of quills. The porcupine flicked out its tail again, and again the big cat squalled. She brushed her nose with her paws, trying to remove the fiery darts. Then she sprang away, squalling with every leap.

One Eye ventured forth. The porcupine had begun to roll up in a ball again. But its muscles were badly ripped and it was bleeding. Its long teeth gave one final clash. Then all the quills drooped down. The porcupine's body relaxed and moved no more.

One Eye studied it for a moment. He took a careful grip of the tender belly with his teeth. He started off, partly carrying, partly dragging the porcupine. When he reached the grouse, he ate it. Then he again took up the porcupine and dragged it back to the hungry she-wolf with her five cubs.

When he dragged the meat into the cave, the she-wolf looked it over. Then she turned her muzzle to One Eye and lightly licked him on the neck. But the next instant, she was warning him away from the cubs with a snarl.

Chapter 5

THE GRAY CUB

He was different from his brothers and sisters. Their hair had some of the reddish color of their mother, the she-wolf. He was the only one who looked like his father. He was the one little gray cub of the litter. He had mostly slept the first month of his life, but now he stayed awake more. His eyes had been open for a week. He was coming to learn his world quite well.

He was a fierce little cub. So were his brothers and sisters. It was to be expected. He came from a breed of meat-killers and meat-eaters. His father and mother lived upon meat. He had lived on milk for a month, but now was ready for meat.

He grew faster than his two brothers and two sisters. He was the first to learn the trick of rolling a fellow cub over. He was the first to grip another cub by the ear. And he certainly caused the mother the most trouble in keeping her cubs from the mouth of the cave.

Like most creatures of the Wild, he learned what it was like to go hungry. There came a time when there was no more meat, and the mother wolf could no longer make milk. At first, the cubs whimpered and cried—but mostly they slept. In time, only one sister and the gray cub lived. But the sister no longer lifted her head nor moved about. Food finally came, but too late for her.

Then there came a time when the gray cub no longer saw his father. The she-wolf knew why One Eye never came back, but had no way to explain that to the gray cub. When she had gone hunting for meat, she had followed a day-old trail of One Eye. And she had found him—and the signs of a battle with a lynx. The lynx had won. Before she went away, the she-wolf followed the tracks to the lynx's den. The signs told her that the lynx was inside with kittens. The she-wolf had not dared to go in.

By the time his mother began leaving the cave to hunt, the cub had learned about fear. He knew he must never go to the white wall of the cave where light shone in. When his mother was away, he slept most of the time. While he was awake he kept very quiet, with no whimpering.

Once, lying awake, he heard a strange sound. He did not know that it was a wolverine, standing outside, sniffing at the cave. The cub only knew that the sniff was strange and unknown. The cub lay still and silent—frozen with fear. When his mother came back, she growled as she smelled the wolverine's track. She bounded into the cave and licked and nuzzled her cub.

Fear kept the cub away from the white wall of light. But as the cub grew, his courage also grew. A wolf cub must know fear, but he must also grow—and learn—and put aside that fear so that he can explore his world. And so, one day the cub's fear was put aside by the rush of life. He stumbled and sprawled toward the white wall.

It was confusing to him. Fear told him to stay back. Something else drove him on. Soon he was at the mouth of the cave. He crouched down and gazed out on the world beyond the wall.

The wall opened out into a great light. Outside he saw things strange to his eyes. Trees. A stream. Huge mountains. And a blue sky high above that. The cub's hair stood on end. He wrinkled his lip and was ready to snarl at whatever came at him.

Nothing happened. He kept looking out, and forgot to snarl. Also, he forgot to be afraid, and he became curious.

Now, the gray cub had lived all his days on a flat floor. He had never been hurt in a fall. So he stepped boldly out upon the air. He fell forward from the cave onto his nose. Fear came back to him! He ki-yi'd like a frightened puppy as he rolled over and over and came to a stop at the bottom of the slope.

He sat up and looked about—and his curiosity returned. He inspected the grass, the plants, and a dead trunk of a pine tree. A squirrel hopped over and gave him a great fright. He snarled, and the squirrel ran for the pine tree.

Now the cub felt brave! When a moosebird rudely hopped up to him, the cub reached out at it with a playful paw. But the bird gave the cub a sharp peck on his nose that made him yelp. The bird quickly flew away.

He traveled very clumsily, but with every mishap he was learning. He was learning about the world and how to get around in it. He figured out that there were live things that moved, and not-alive things that did not move. He watched out for the live things.

The cub was born to be a hunter of meat, although he did not know it. He happened upon meat just outside his own cave door on this first adventure beyond the wall of white. It was by luck that he tripped and fell into the hidden grouse nest and found himself in a nest with seven chicks.

They made noises, and at first he was frightened. Then he placed his paw on one. He smelled it. He picked it up in his mouth. His jaws closed together. The taste of it was good. So he ate the grouse. Soon he had eaten the whole brood. The mother grouse arrived in a fury and he hid his head between his paws and yelped. Then he became angry. He sank his tiny teeth into one of her wings and pulled her into the open. The grouse struggled against the cub, but the cub was just doing what he was made for—killing meat and battling to kill it.

WHITE FANG

After a time, the bird stopped struggling. The cub still held her by the wing, and they lay on the ground and looked at each other. He tried to growl ferociously. She pecked on his nose. He winced— and began to whimper. He tried to back away, but he still held the grouse. A rain of pecks followed. The cub released the bird, then turned tail and scampered off. Once more, a fear of this unknown world rushed upon him. He shrank back into the shelter of a bush. Just then he felt a breeze of air fan him. A large, winged body swept silently past. A hawk, diving down out of the blue, had barely missed him.

It was a long time before the cub left his shelter and explored the stream. Not knowing better, he stepped boldly out onto the water—and went down! He came to the surface, and the sweet air rushed into his open mouth. He began to swim naturally. The near bank was only a yard away, but he had come up with his back to it. The first thing he saw was the opposite bank. Midway across, the current picked up the cub and swept him downstream. The quiet water became suddenly angry. Sometimes he was under, sometimes on top, sometimes smashing against the rocks.

Below the rapids was a pool of calm water. Here the water gently carried him toward the bank. He frantically crawled clear of the water. As he was scrambling between some bushes, he saw a flash of yellow. A long, lean weasel was leaping swiftly away from him. Then, at his feet, he saw a very small thing, only several inches long. It was a young weasel that had gone out adventuring, just like himself. The cub turned it over with his paw. Suddenly, yellow flashed again before his eyes! At the same instant he felt the sharp teeth of the mother weasel cut into his flesh. While he yelped, he saw the mother weasel grab her young one and disappear with it into the thicket.

The cub was still whimpering when the mother weasel returned. She came closer—and then her teeth were at his throat! The gray cub would have died—and there would have been no story to write about him—had the she-wolf not come bounding through the bushes. The weasel let go of the cub and flashed at the she-wolf's throat. It missed, catching hold on the jaw instead. The she-wolf whipped her head, flinging the weasel high in the air. And, still in the air, the she-wolf's jaws closed on the lean, yellow body.

WHITE FANG

The cub rested for two days, and then went out again. But on this trip he did not get lost. When he grew tired, he made his way back to the cave, and slept. Everyday after this, he made his way out and explored a wider area.

He grew and learned quickly. He learned when to be bold, and when to be cautious. The chatter of the squirrels no longer frightened him. But the shadow of the hawk sent him crouching into the nearest thicket.

The cub respected his mother. She could get meat, and she always brought him his share. She was unafraid of things. She had experience and knowledge, and to the cub this was power.

But meat became scarce again, and hunger and famine returned. The she-wolf ran herself thin hunting for meat. She rarely slept anymore in the cave. She spent most of her time on the meat-trail—and rarely found meat. This famine was not a long one, but it was hard while it lasted. The mother could no longer make milk for the cub, and she had no meat to bring him. The cub tried to chase down squirrels and dig mice out of their burrows. But he did not succeed. He crawled off to whimper out of hunger.

WHITE FANG

Finally, one day the she-wolf brought home meat. It was strange meat, different from any she had ever brought before. It was a lynx kitten, partly grown, like the cub, but not so large. And it was all for him. His mother had already eaten another lynx kitten. The cub did not know that this would put them in danger. He only knew that he was hungry—and here was meat. He ate and grew happier with every mouthful.

After eating, the cub fell asleep against his mother's side. Her snarling woke him. The cub looked up and saw, crouching in the entrance of the cave, the lynx mother.

The lynx tried to rush into the den, but the she-wolf sprang upon her. There was a tremendous snarling and spitting and screeching.

Once, the cub sprang in and sank his teeth into the hind-leg of the lynx. The next moment, the two mothers separated and the lynx lashed out at the cub, but that did not stop him. At the end of the battle, the cub was again clinging to a hind-leg and growling between his teeth.

The lynx mother was dead, but the she-wolf had been greatly injured. For more than a day she lay still. For a week she never left the cave,

WHITE FANG

except for water, and she moved slowly and painfully. At the end of that time they had finished eating the lynx. The she-wolf's wounds had healed enough for her to hunt again.

The cub began to hunt with his mother. He saw much of the killing and began to play his part in it. And he learned: *Life lived on life.* There were the eaters and the eaten. The law was: *Eat or be eaten.*

The world was full of surprise, and the cub learned to obey the laws of nature. The stir of life was in him. His muscles grew stronger. Running down meat was a thrill. Battles were pleasures. It was a joy to have a full stomach and doze lazily in the sunshine. This was all a part of life. He was very much alive, very happy, and very proud of himself.

Chapter 6

THE MAKERS OF FIRE

The cub came upon them suddenly. He had left the cave and run down to the stream to drink. He was trotting past the trees, and in one instant he saw and smelt. Before him were five live things he had never seen before. They did not move, but sat there on their haunches, silent. Nor did the cub move. He was in awe. He had never seen man, but he sensed their mastery and power.

One of the Indians arose and walked over to him. The cub cowered to the ground. As the Indian reached out a hand, the cub bared his fangs. The hand paused and the man laughed. *"Wabam wabisca ip pit tah."* ("Look! The white fangs!")

The other Indians laughed loudly, and urged the man to pick up the cub. As the hand came down, the cub's teeth sank into it. The next moment, the cub received a slap alongside the head that knocked him over on his side. He sat up on his haunches and ki-yi'd.

The four Indians laughed more loudly. Even the man who had been bitten began to laugh. Then the cub heard something, and knew what it was. He gave a last, long wail, and waited for the coming of his mother.

She bounded in amongst them, snarling as she ran. He bounded to meet her, while the man-animals quickly stepped back.

Then a cry went up from one of the men:

"Kiche!"

The cub felt his mother wilting at the sound. The she-wolf, the fearless one, crouched down till her belly touched the ground. She whimpered, wagged her tail, and made signs of peace. The men surrounded her, and felt her, and petted her.

"It is a year, Gray Beaver, since Kiche ran away," spoke an Indian.

"Yes—the year of the famine. There was no meat for the dogs. She is part wolf, so she left to live with the wolves. This be the sign of it," Gray Beaver answered. He laid his hand on the cub. The cub snarled a little at the touch of the hand.

"There is in him little dog and much wolf," Gray Beaver went on. "His fangs be white, and White Fang shall be his name."

White Fang watched as the man-animal tied a string of rawhide around his mother's throat. Then the man-animal led her to a small pine tree, where he tied the other end of the string. White Fang followed and lay down beside her. Another man-animal reached down to pet White Fang. White Fang snarled, but soon gave way as the hand rolled him over, rubbed his belly playfully, and tickled behind his ears. Then the man left him alone and went away. All fear had died out of White Fang.

After a time, White Fang heard new noises coming. He knew them at once for man-animal noises. A few minutes later the whole tribe trailed in—more men and many women and children, all carrying heavy camp equipment. Also there were many dogs and part-grown puppies. The grown dogs carried bags of thirty to forty pounds on their backs, fastened underneath.

White Fang had never seen dogs before. They were like his own kind, but somehow different. Suddenly, they attacked! White Fang could hear the snarl of Kiche as she fought for him. He could hear the cries of the man-animals, the sound of clubs striking upon bodies, and the yelps of pain from the dogs.

Within a few seconds he was on his feet again. He could now see the man-animals driving back the dogs with clubs and stones, saving him from the savage teeth of his kind that somehow was not his kind.

So much was new to White Fang. These man-animals who had a power—like gods. This new pack of animals that treated him cruelly. Before, he had only known One Eye, his mother, and himself. And now he resented that these, his kind, had tried to destroy him. He resented his mother being tied. This kept her away from him, and he was still in need of his mother's side. He no longer was free. And he did not like it.

The Indians arose and went on their march. A boy took the end of the rope and led Kiche. White Fang followed. They went down the valley to where the stream met the Mackenzie River.

Here, there were canoes stored on poles high in the air, and fish-racks for the drying of fish. The men set up the camp and built great tepees.

White Fang's mother was tied to a peg and he strayed away from her. A part-grown puppy came toward him slowly. The puppy's name, as White Fang later heard him called, was Lip-lip. White Fang prepared to meet him in friendly spirit. But suddenly, with remarkable swiftness, Lip-lip leaped in. Three times, four times, and half a dozen times, his sharp little teeth scored on the newcomer. Yelping in shame, White Fang fled to the side of his mother. Kiche licked him tenderly.

Before long, White Fang's curiosity returned, and he was venturing forth again. Gray Beaver was squatting and doing something with sticks and dry moss on the ground. White Fang came near to him and watched. He saw a strange thing like mist arise from the sticks beneath Gray Beaver's hands. He crawled several steps forward until his nose touched the flame. At the same instant his little tongue went out to it.

He scrambled backward, bursting in ki-yi's. Gray Beaver laughed loudly, and slapped his thighs. Soon everybody was laughing!

WHITE FANG

It was the worst hurt he had ever known. His nose and tongue were scorched. He cried hopelessly as the men laughed. And then the shame came to him. He now knew laughter and what it meant. And he felt shame that the man-animals were laughing at him. He turned and fled, not from the hurt of the fire, but from the laughter that sank even deeper. He fled to Kiche, the one creature in the world who was not laughing at him.

Night came, and White Fang lay by his mother's side. His nose and tongue still hurt. But worse than this, he was homesick. The only life he had known was gone.

He did not understand these man-animals. They held powers he did not hold. They could make dead things—stones and sticks—obey them. They could make sun-colored life spring from wood and moss. They were fire-makers! They were gods!

---— *Chapter 7* ———

LIFE AT CAMP

While Kiche was tied by the stick, White Fang ran about the camp. He came to know the ways of the man-animals and their god-like powers. When they walked, he got out of their way. When they called, he came. When they were angry, he crouched down. When they commanded him to go, he obeyed. He learned about clubs and flying stones and stinging lashes of whips. He belonged to them as all dogs belonged to them.

But there were days when he crept to the edge of the forest and stood and listened to something calling him far and away. Yet always he returned, to whimper softly at Kiche's side.

JACK LONDON

The curse of his life was Lip-lip. He was a bully—larger, older, and stronger than White Fang. Lip-lip became a nightmare to him. Whenever White Fang slipped away from his mother, Lip-lip appeared. He trailed at White Fang's heels, snarling, picking on him. He would not allow White Fang to play with the other puppies at camp. He waited until no man-animals were around. Then he would spring upon White Fang and force a fight. Lip-lip always won.

Still, White Fang did not lose his spirit. Instead, he became more savage. He lost his playful, puppyish ways. He became more cunning in order to survive at camp. Lip-lip kept White Fang from his share of food, so White Fang became a clever thief. He learned to sneak about camp, to know what was going on everywhere, and to avoid Lip-lip.

The day came when Gray Beaver untied Kiche from the stick. White Fang was delighted with his mother's freedom. He walked with her joyfully about the camp. As long as he remained close by her side, Lip-lip kept his distance.

Later that day, White Fang led his mother, and they strayed off to the edge of the woods.

JACK LONDON

The stream, the cave, and the quiet forest were calling to him, and he wanted her to come. He ran on a few steps, stopped, and looked back. She had not moved. He whined. She only turned her head and gazed back at the camp.

There was something calling to him out there in the open. His mother heard it, too. But she heard also that other and louder call, the call of the fire and of man.

Kiche turned and slowly trotted back toward camp. White Fang whimpered. He was only a part-grown puppy. For him, there was still something stronger than the call of man or of the Wild. This was the call of his mother. So he arose and trotted sadly back to camp.

But White Fang's time with his mother was short. Gray Beaver was in debt to Three Eagles, who was going away on a trip up the Mackenzie River. Gray Beaver gave him a strip of scarlet cloth, a bearskin, and Kiche to pay the debt. White Fang saw his mother taken aboard Three Eagles' canoe, and tried to follow her. A blow from Three Eagles knocked him backward to the land. The canoe shoved off. He sprang into the water and swam after her!

Gray Beaver angrily came after White Fang in a canoe. He reached down and, by the nape of the neck, lifted him clear of the water. He threw him into the bottom of the canoe and gave him a beating until White Fang could no longer stand.

When the canoe touched the shore, Gray Beaver flung White Fang, whimpering, onto the rocks. Lip-lip now rushed upon him. White Fang was too helpless to defend himself. He would have been badly hurt had Gray Beaver not kicked at Lip-lip. And so White Fang learned that only the gods had the right to punish.

That night, White Fang cried for his mother. Gray Beaver, awakened by White Fang's cries, beat him again. He cried no more around the gods. But sometimes, he would stray to the edge of the woods by himself and cry out with loud whimperings. For now he was alone.

He could have run back to the Wild, but the memory of his mother held him to camp. Sometimes Three Eagles visited the camp with Kiche. So White Fang stayed—always waiting for her. Before long, he had learned how to get along with Gray Beaver. The man-animal never petted him, but he fed him and defended him.

Lip-lip, however, kept bullying him. The young dogs followed Lip-lip's lead. White Fang could whip many of them one-on-one, but a fight was a signal for all the young dogs in camp to come running. When White Fang did win, the man-animals beat him. This made White Fang more ferocious. He became an outcast, and a sneak and a troublemaker. But he learned how to take care of himself in a mass fight. He became cat-like in his ability to stay on his feet. Grown dogs could hurtle him backward, but he always went with his legs under him and his feet to the earth, ready to spring forward or away.

White Fang learned to attack quickly. If he could take a dog by surprise, the dog was already half-whipped.

The pack would not allow White Fang to run with them. And White Fang would attack any dog that was alone. The young dogs, except for Lip-lip, became afraid to run by themselves. But the pack would go after White Fang and hunt him as he ran—and lost them—through the woods.

In time, man and dog both hated White Fang. The tooth of every dog was against him, the hand of every man. He was alert for any attack.

He was hated by his own kind and mankind. But he learned how to survive. He learned to obey the strong and to go after the weak. Gray Beaver was the strong. Therefore White Fang obeyed him. But any dog younger or smaller than himself was weak, a thing to be destroyed. He became quicker than the other dogs, swifter of foot, craftier, deadlier, more lean with iron-like muscle. He was more cruel, more ferocious, and more intelligent. He had to become all these things, or he would not have survived in the world in which he found himself.

Chapter 8

CHANGES AND NEW LAWS

In the fall, the summer camp was taken down. The tribe was preparing to go off to the fall hunting grounds. White Fang watched it all. When the tepees began to come down and the canoes were loading at the bank, he understood. He crawled into the dense thicket and waited.

He heard Gray Beaver calling him by name, but he did not move. The voices died away and darkness came. For a while he played among the trees, enjoying his freedom. Then, suddenly, he was aware of loneliness. He became frightened. He felt cold. Here was no warm side of a tepee against which to snuggle. Here was no meat.

White Fang had forgotten how to take care of himself. A panic seized him, and he ran madly toward the village. He passed out of the forest and into the moonlit open. But no village greeted his eyes. The man-animals had moved on— without him.

He slunk sadly through the deserted camp, smelling the rubbish heaps. He would have been glad just to hear the rattle of stones being flung his way. He would have been happy to see Gray Beaver. He longed to see Lip-lip and the whole snarling pack again.

He came to where Gray Beaver's tepee had stood. There he sat down. He pointed his nose at the moon. With a heart-broken cry, filled with loneliness and grief for Kiche, he howled a long wolf-howl. It was his first howl.

When daylight came, he plunged back into the forest to search for the trail of the gods. All day he ran. He did not rest. By the middle of the second day, he had been running for thirty hours. He had not eaten in forty hours, and he was weak with hunger. His handsome coat was draggled. His feet were bruised and bleeding. He had begun to limp. To make it worse, snow began to fall.

WHITE FANG

Night had fallen when White Fang limped across a fresh-smelling trail in the snow. He knew it immediately for what it was! He hurried along the trail and came into the new camp. There was Gray Beaver, crouching by the fire.

White Fang was afraid of the beating he'd get from Gray Beaver. But he also knew how safe and warm he would be near his fire once more—even with the other hated dogs. White Fang crawled slowly toward Gray Beaver, waiting for his punishment.

Gray Beaver put out his hand—but he did not hit White Fang. Instead, he offered him a piece of fresh meat. After that, White Fang lay at Gray Beaver's feet, gazing at the fire that warmed him.

In December, Gray Beaver went on a journey up the Mackenzie River. Mit-sah and Kloo-kooch—Gray Beaver's son and wife—went with him. Gray Beaver drove one sled himself. Mit-sah drove a smaller sled with a team of seven puppies. Most were nine and ten months old, but White Fang was only eight months old.

Mit-sah looked like his father, and had much of his father's wisdom. He was aware that Lip-lip bullied White Fang, but Lip-lip had been another man's dog. His father had done some trading, and now Lip-lip was Mit-sah's dog. He placed Lip-lip at the end of the longest rope. This made Lip-lip the leader. But instead of being bully and master of the pack, Lip-lip now found himself hated by the pack. The moment the sled started, the team took after Lip-lip in a chase that lasted the whole day. Even though Lip-lip was the head dog, he was no longer "leader" among the other puppies.

White Fang enjoyed the work. He worked hard, learned discipline, and was obedient. Still, he stayed to himself. He had never learned to play. Since Lip-lip no longer ruled the others, White Fang could have become leader of the pack. But he just wanted to be left alone. They knew to get out of his way when he came along. Even the boldest of them would never dare to rob him of his meat. In fact, they quickly ate their own meat, for fear that he would take it away from them. White Fang knew the law well:

Oppress the Weak. Obey the Strong.

The months passed by. White Fang grew stronger with the long hours on the trail and the steady toil at the sled. He had come to know the world as a fierce and brutal place. He had no love for Gray Beaver. He respected him and obeyed him, but he felt no love. If Gray Beaver had given him a kind word, or a gentle touch, White Fang might have felt something deeper for this god. But Gray Beaver did not pet him nor speak kind words. It was not his way.

So White Fang knew nothing of the kindness a man's hand might offer. Besides, he did not like the hands of the man-animals. He did not trust them. It was true they sometimes gave him meat, but more often they gave hurt. Hands were things to keep away from. They hurled stones, held clubs and sticks and whips. In strange villages that they came to, White Fang stayed away from hands—especially those of children, who could pinch and hurt.

In a village at the Great Lake, White Fang learned a new law: *Never bite one of the gods*. A boy was chopping frozen moose-meat. White Fang stopped and began to eat the small pieces that flew off into the snow. The boy laid down his axe,

took up a club, and chased White Fang between two tepees. He trapped White Fang against a high earth bank. White Fang was furious. He had done no wrong! One thing led to the next, and the boy somehow found himself on his back. His club-hand was bleeding where White Fang had bitten him. Then White Fang knew he had done wrong.

White Fang fled away to Gray Beaver and crouched behind his legs. When the boy's family came, they demanded that the dog be punished. But Gray Beaver, Mit-sah, and Kloo-kooch defended him. White Fang had learned that to bite a god was wrong—but that not all gods were allowed to punish him.

Before the day was out, White Fang learned a new law: *Protect your own.* Mit-sah was gathering firewood in the forest when he was attacked by a gang of boys. They were led by the boy who had been bitten. White Fang looked on. One of his own gods was being hurt! Anger filled him and he jumped to Mit-sah's defense. Five minutes later, the gang of boys had fled. When Mit-sah told his story in camp, Gray Beaver ordered meat to be given to White Fang. White Fang knew he was being rewarded for his protection of the pack.

In the days that followed, White Fang learned more about protecting his pack and his pack's property. Gray Beaver trained him to protect them from thieves. He became a guard dog—and no man and no other dog could get past him. In return, White Fang was rewarded with food and the warmth of the fire.

The bond between man and dog grew stronger as the months went by. White Fang did his duty to protect his own. He felt awe and respect for his gods. But he did not feel love. He did not know what love was. The memory of his mother, Kiche, slowly left him. His bond to the man-animals became stronger than a need for freedom—and his old home in the Wild.

Chapter 9

THE FAMINE

In April, Gray Beaver returned to the summer village. White Fang was now a year old. Though still not fully grown, he was larger than the others his age—except for Lip-lip. And he was intelligent. His strong build came from his wolf father, and his mental strength from his half-dog mother.

The man-animals cut up a large moose, giving parts to the dogs. White Fang got a hoof and part of the shinbone with quite a bit of meat attached. He was eating his prize when Baseek, an old dog, rushed in upon him. White Fang slashed back at him, and Baseek stepped back in surprise. The meaty shinbone lay between them.

Baseek bristled fiercely and snarled across the shinbone. White Fang felt small, and looked for a way to escape. But then Baseek made his mistake. He still thought of White Fang as just a pup and himself as the strong bully. He stepped forward to the meat.

This was too much for White Fang. He could not stand by while another took what belonged to him. He struck without warning and Baseek was knocked off his feet. His throat was bitten. His ear ripped. His shoulder torn. The swiftness of it was bewildering.

The situation was now reversed. White Fang stood over the shinbone and snarled at Baseek. Baseek calmly retreated.

White Fang had stood his ground against a full-grown dog. He now walked proudly among the dogs. The older dogs quickly learned that if they left him alone, he left them alone.

In midsummer, White Fang was trotting along the edge of the village when he came upon Kiche. He paused and looked at her. He began to remember her, but she did not remember him. She lifted her lip in a snarl—and then the old memories rushed back to him. He bounded

toward her joyously, but she met him with sharp fangs. He did not understand. He backed slowly away, puzzled.

But it was not Kiche's fault. A wolf mother was not made to remember her cubs of a year or so before. So she did not remember White Fang. He was now a strange animal. She had a new litter of puppies to guard.

White Fang looked at Kiche licking one of her new puppies. There was no place for her in his life anymore. There was no place for him in hers. Kiche snarled once more at him, and White Fang walked away.

The months went by and White Fang grew stronger and heavier. He had only one weakness. He could not stand being laughed at. It so outraged him that for hours he would behave like a demon, racing about and attacking other dogs.

In the third year of his life, a great famine came to the Mackenzie Indians. In the summer the fish failed. In the winter the caribou and moose were scarce. The rabbits almost disappeared. Only the strong survived. The old and weak died of hunger. There was wailing in the village as all went hungry.

A few of the boldest and wisest dogs fled into the forest. There, in the end, they starved to death or were eaten by wolves.

In this time of misery, White Fang also stole away into the woods. Unlike the other dogs, he had learned the ways of the woods in his cubhood. He hunted out squirrels and wood mice, patiently and cunningly. He even robbed one of Gray Beaver's rabbit snares.

He journeyed over to the valley and stream where he had been born. Here, in the old cave, he came upon Kiche. She, too, had fled the camp and had given birth to more puppies. Only one puppy remained alive. White Fang looked in, then left and trotted on up the stream. He found the old hiding place of the lynx that he and his mother had fought long before. Here he settled down and rested for a day.

During the early summer, he met Lip-lip, who had also taken to the woods. Trotting in opposite directions around a high bluff, they each rounded a corner of rock and found themselves face to face. Lip-lip learned too late that small cubs soon grow up, and that they remember. White Fang left him dead by the stream.

One day, not long after, White Fang came to the edge of the forest. Here a narrow stretch of open land sloped down to the Mackenzie River. He paused to study the situation. Familiar sights, sounds, and scents called to him. It was the old village changed to a new place. And there was a smell in the air of fish. There was food. The famine was gone. He came out boldly from the forest and trotted straight to Gray Beaver's tepee. Gray Beaver was not there, but Kloo-kooch welcomed him with glad cries and fresh fish. He lay down to wait for Gray Beaver.

Chapter 10

THE ENEMY OF HIS KIND

With Lip-lip gone, Mit-sah made White Fang the new leader of the sled team. This made the dogs hate him. They hated him when Mit-sah gave him extra meat. They hated him because he seemed to receive special favors. And they hated him because he was always at the head of their team—fleeing just out of reach.

And White Fang hated them back. He hated being at the head of the yelling pack. He hated running away from the dogs he had defeated for the past three years. And if he turned upon them, Mit-sah would throw the stinging lash of the whip into his face.

White Fang could only slow down when Mit-sah cried out for the team to stop. At first this caused trouble for the other dogs. They would attack White Fang only to be hit with the whip by Mit-sah. So the dogs came to understand that when Mit-sah gave the order to stop, White Fang was to be let alone. But when White Fang stopped without orders, then they were allowed to spring upon him.

The dogs learned that it was best to keep together. White Fang was too terrible for any of them to face alone. He was too quick for them, too big, too wise. Unlike the other dogs, he still had the Wild in him. He was the enemy of his own kind. Gray Beaver could not help but admire and marvel at White Fang.

When White Fang was nearly five years old, Gray Beaver took him on another journey. In many of the villages along the way, White Fang attacked the strange dogs. They were ordinary dogs. They were not prepared for his swiftness. They growled, but White Fang wasted no time growling. He was at their throats before they knew what was happening. He was a skilled fighter. The dogs had no chance against him.

It was in the summer that White Fang and Gray Beaver arrived at Fort Yukon. Gray Beaver had crossed between the Mackenzie and the Yukon rivers in the late winter. He spent the spring hunting along the western Rockies. He waited for the ice to break up on the Porcupine River. Then he had built a canoe and paddled down that stream to meet the Yukon River just under the Arctic Circle. It was the summer of 1898. Thousands of gold-hunters were going up the Yukon. Some had even come from the other side of the world.

Here Gray Beaver stopped. A whisper of the gold rush had reached his ears. He had come with several bales of furs, mittens, and moccasins to trade. It was a good trip. He made more profit than he expected.

It was at Fort Yukon that White Fang saw his first white men. They had houses and a huge fort of logs. For the first few hours he was content with slinking around and watching them from a safe distance. The white men also watched White Fang with great curiosity. They pointed him out to one another. When they came near him, he showed his teeth and backed away.

Every two or three days, a steamboat stopped at the bank for several hours. The white men came off these steamers and went away on them again. White Fang was cautious with the white men, but not with their dogs. He was an enemy of all dogs. All he had to do, when the strange dogs came ashore, was to show himself. They rushed at him from off the ships out of instinct. But these dogs were soft and helpless. White Fang sprang to the side, confusing the dogs. In that moment he struck them on the shoulder, rolling them off their feet and going for the throat. The pack would rush in and finish killing the dog, while White Fang ran to safety.

It was then that the white men rushed in. White Fang would stand off at a little distance and look on, while stones, clubs, axes, and all sorts of weapons fell upon the other dogs. White Fang enjoyed it all. He did not love his own kind. He hated all dogs—those of the Indians, and those of the white men.

How could White Fang have turned out any other way? He had seen the first light of day in a lonely cave. He had fought his first fights in the Wild—with the grouse, the weasel, and the lynx.

His puppyhood had been made bitter by the bullying of Lip-lip and the whole puppy pack. If Lip-lip had never existed, White Fang might have grown up happily with the other puppies. He would have become more doglike, with more liking for dogs. If Gray Beaver had shown just a little love, White Fang might have turned out more trusting and kind. But these things had not been so. The world molded White Fang until he became what he was. He was unloving and ferocious. He was the enemy of all his kind.

Chapter 11

BEAUTY SMITH

The few white men who lived in Fort Yukon had been there a long time. They made fun of the newcomers who arrived on the steamers and enjoyed seeing them make mistakes. And they enjoyed seeing the newcomers' dogs being "met" at the docks by White Fang and the other camp dogs. It was a sport to watch the dogs fight.

There was one man who particularly enjoyed the sport. He would come running at the first sound of a steamboat's whistle. When a soft newcomer's dog went down, he cried out with delight. He stayed until the last fight was over, and White Fang and the pack had scattered.

The other men called this man "Beauty" Smith. But he was anything but a beauty. He did the cooking for the other men in the fort, the dishwashing and the unpleasant work. And the men feared him. He was weak and cowardly—and this made him cruel and disliked.

Beauty Smith kept a sharp eye on White Fang. This was an animal he wanted to own. White Fang didn't like the man. He sensed evil in him.

White Fang was in Gray Beaver's camp when Beauty Smith first visited. Gray Beaver refused to sell the dog. He had grown rich with his trading and needed nothing. But Beauty Smith visited Gray Beaver's camp often, and hidden under his coat was always a bottle of whiskey. Each time he tried to buy White Fang, he shared his bottle. Gray Beaver started buying whiskey—and grew to crave the taste. It was not long before Gray Beaver's money was gone. Nothing remained but his thirst for whiskey. Beauty Smith talked with him again about the sale of White Fang. But this time the price offered was in bottles, not dollars, and Gray Beaver's ears were eager.

White Fang slunk into camp one evening, tired but content. But he had scarcely lain down when Gray Beaver staggered over to him. He tied a leather strap around his neck. An hour passed and Beauty Smith strode into camp and stood over White Fang. One hand began to come down upon the dog's head. White Fang's snarl grew tense and harsh. Suddenly he snapped, striking with his fangs like a snake. The hand was jerked back. Beauty Smith was frightened and angry. Gray Beaver clouted White Fang alongside the head, so that he lay down obediently.

Beauty Smith went away and returned with a stout club. Then Gray Beaver gave over the end of the strap, and Beauty Smith started to walk away. White Fang resisted. Gray Beaver hit him to make him follow. White Fang rushed forward, hurling himself upon Beauty. Beauty Smith did not jump away. He was expecting this. He swung the club smartly, sending White Fang to the ground. Gray Beaver laughed. Beauty Smith tightened the strap again, and White Fang crawled limply and dizzily to his feet. He did not rush a second time. He followed at Beauty Smith's heels, his tail between his legs, and snarling under his breath.

At the fort, Beauty Smith left him tied outside. In ten seconds, White Fang chewed through the leather and hurried back to Gray Beaver's camp.

Gray Beaver again put a leash on him, and in the morning turned him over to Beauty Smith, who gave him a beating. Club and whip were both used upon him. It was the worst beating White Fang had known in his life.

Beauty Smith enjoyed the task as he swung the whip and club, and listened to White Fang's helpless cries. For Beauty Smith was cruel in the way that cowards are cruel. They can't be men to men, but must be brutes to anything weaker than themselves.

After the beating, Beauty Smith dragged White Fang back to the fort and tied him to a stick. During the night, White Fang again chewed free and went back to Gray Beaver. But he was betrayed yet a third time. And this time he was beaten even more severely than before.

White Fang was dragged again to the fort and was now tied with a chain. After a few days, Gray Beaver left to return to the Mackenzie. White Fang remained on the Yukon. He now belonged to a man more than half mad and all brute.

WHITE FANG

White Fang was chained in a pen at the back of the fort. Here Beauty Smith teased and irritated him. The man discovered White Fang's hatred of laughter, and made it a point to trick him and then laugh at him.

White Fang had now become an enemy and hater of *all* things. He hated the chain around his neck. He hated the men who looked in at him through the slats of the pen. He hated the dogs that snarled at him. He hated the very wood of the pen that held him. And first, last, and most of all, he hated Beauty Smith.

But Beauty Smith had a purpose in all that he did. One day a number of men gathered about the pen. Beauty Smith entered, club in hand, and took the chain off White Fang's neck. White Fang tore around the inside of the pen. The men admired him. He was bigger than the average wolf. He was all muscle—ninety pounds of fighting fury.

The door of the pen was opened again. White Fang paused. Then a huge dog—a mastiff—was thrust inside, and the door was slammed shut. The mastiff sprung, but White Fang leaped in with a flash of fangs that ripped at the dog's neck.

The men outside shouted and applauded. Beauty Smith was delighted with White Fang's fighting ability. There was no hope for the mastiff from the start. In the end, the dead mastiff was dragged out by its owner. Then there was a payment of bets, and money clinked in Beauty Smith's hand.

White Fang came to look forward to when men gathered around his pen. It meant a fight. One day he fought three dogs in a row. Once he fought two dogs at once. He was always the victor.

In the fall of the year, Beauty Smith bought tickets for himself and White Fang on a steamboat bound up the Yukon. White Fang was known far and wide as "The Fighting Wolf." Men stared at him, poked sticks between the bars of his cage on the ship, and then laughed at him.

When the steamboat arrived at Dawson, White Fang went ashore. Men paid fifty cents in gold dust just to see "The Fighting Wolf." He was given no rest. Whenever he lay down to sleep, he was stirred up by a sharp stick—so that the audience might get its money's worth. He was kept in a rage most of the time, and was called the most fearsome of wild beasts.

WHITE FANG

When a fight was arranged, he was taken out of his cage at night and led off into the woods a few miles from town to avoid the police. He always won his matches. He was fast, he rushed in quickly, and he was experienced. He knew more about fighting than any dog that faced him. In time, no one would pit his dog against White Fang. Beauty drew a crowd when he had White Fang fight a wild wolf. Once, he tossed in a full-grown female lynx. White Fang fought for his life.

After the lynx, all fighting stopped for White Fang. There were no more animals to pit against him. So he remained on exhibition until spring, when Tim Keenan, a card-dealer, arrived in the land. With him came the first bulldog that had ever entered the Klondike. Everyone knew that this dog and White Fang would fight.

With night came horror. The starving wolves were growing bolder.
page 214

White Fang crawled slowly toward Gray Beaver,
waiting for his punishment.
page 276

Tim Keenan shoved the bulldog forward with a muttered, "Go to it."
page 313

It was Weedon Scott's patience and love that changed White Fang.
page 330

Chapter 12

THE CLINGING DEATH

Beauty Smith slipped the chain from White Fang's neck and stepped back.

For once White Fang did not make an immediate attack. He had never seen such a dog before. Tim Keenan shoved the bulldog forward with a muttered, "Go to it." The dog waddled toward the center of the circle. He stopped and blinked at White Fang.

There were cries from the crowd of "Go to him, Cherokee!" "Eat him up!"

But Cherokee did not seem anxious to fight. He turned and blinked at the men and wagged his stump of a tail. He was not afraid—just lazy.

313

Tim Keenan stepped in and bent over the bulldog, giving him another shove forward. Then White Fang struck. A cry of startled admiration went up from the crowd.

The bulldog was bleeding behind one ear from a rip in his thick neck. He gave no sign of pain, did not even snarl, but turned and followed after White Fang. The bulldog's bowlegged, steady walk and White Fang's quickness excited the crowd. The men were making new bets. Again, and yet again, White Fang sprang in and got away untouched. Still the strange dog waddled after him.

White Fang was puzzled. He had never seen such a dog. It was soft and slow and gave no cry. White Fang could never get at the soft underside of the throat. The bulldog stood too short, and its huge jaws were in the way. Those same jaws were patiently waiting to get a grip on White Fang.

The time went by. White Fang dodged and danced about, striking again and again. The bulldog's ears had been torn, his neck and shoulders were slashed, and his very lips were cut and bleeding. Still he wagged his stumpy tail and blinked at the men. He was just waiting—waiting to get his own grip on White Fang's throat.

Time and again, White Fang tried to knock Cherokee off his feet. But Cherokee was too close to the ground. White Fang tried the trick once too often. One last time he drove in, but his own shoulder was high above Cherokee's. He struck, turned a half-somersault in the air, and went right over the bulldog's body. For the first time, men saw White Fang lose his footing. In that instant, Cherokee's teeth closed on his throat.

It was not a good grip. It was too low down toward the chest, but Cherokee held on. White Fang sprang to his feet and tore wildly around, trying to shake off the bulldog's body. It made him frantic, this clinging, dragging weight. Round and round he went, whirling and turning. The bulldog did little but keep his grip. He knew he was doing the right thing by holding on. The grip was the thing, and the grip he kept.

The bulldog pushed forward and rolled White Fang over on his back, still hanging on to his throat. Slowly it shifted his grip, moving up the throat. Bit by bit, whenever the chance offered, the bulldog slowly choked White Fang. There was no escaping the grip. White Fang could do nothing. The battle would soon be over.

WHITE FANG

Beauty Smith knew how to get White Fang riled. He took a step into the ring and pointed his finger at White Fang. Then he began to laugh. White Fang went wild with rage and gained his feet. Round and round, stumbling and falling, he fought against the clinging death. But at last he fell again. Shouts of applause went up. Cherokee responded by wagging the stump of his tail.

It was at this time that there came a jingle of bells. Everybody, except Beauty Smith, looked up in fear that the police were coming. Two men rode up with sleds and dogs. Seeing the crowd, the men stopped. The dog-musher wore a mustache. The taller, younger man was smooth-shaven.

White Fang had stopped struggling. He could get little air. When Beauty Smith saw White Fang's eyes beginning to glaze, he knew the fight was lost. He sprang upon White Fang in anger and began to kick him. At that moment, the tall, young newcomer forced his way through the crowd and sent his fist into Beauty's face. Beauty Smith seemed to lift into the air as he turned over backward and struck the snow. The newcomer's gray eyes flashed upon the crowd.

"You cowards!" he cried. "You beasts!"

WHITE FANG

Beauty Smith, the coward that he was, lay where he had fallen, making no effort to get up.

"Come on, Matt, lend a hand," the newcomer called to the dog-musher.

Both men bent over the dogs. Matt took hold of White Fang, ready to pull when the tall man could loosen Cherokee's jaws.

The crowd began to grow unruly. The tall man raised his head and glared at them.

"Won't some of you help?" he cried.

No help was offered.

"It's no use, Mr. Scott, you can't break 'em apart that way," Matt said. "You'll need a pry."

Scott tried to thrust the muzzle of his revolver between the bulldog's jaws to pry them open.

Tim Keenan strode into the ring. "Don't break them teeth, stranger."

"Then I'll break his neck," Scott answered.

He managed to get the muzzle in between the jaws on one side and out between the jaws on the other side. He pried gently and carefully, loosening the jaws a bit at a time.

Keenan stooped down and got a firm hold on Cherokee. The dogs were finally pulled apart, though the bulldog continued to struggle.

White Fang made a few attempts to get up. His legs were too weak, and he sank down into the snow. His eyes were half-closed. He looked like a dog that had been strangled to death.

Matt looked him over and said, "Just about done in, but he's breathin'."

"Matt, how much is a good sled dog worth?" Scott asked.

"Three hundred dollars."

"And how much for one that's all chewed up?"

"Half of that."

Scott turned to Beauty Smith. "I'm going to give you a hundred and fifty for him."

"I ain't a-sellin'," Beauty said.

"Oh, yes, you are," the other assured him. "The dog's mine."

"I know my rights," Beauty said fearfully.

"You lost your rights to own that dog. Are you going to take the money? Or do I have to hit you again?"

"All right," said Beauty Smith. "But I'm bein' robbed, and a man's got rights."

"Correct," Scott answered, passing the money over to him. "A man's got rights. But you're not a man. You're a beast."

WHITE FANG

Off to the side, Tim Keenan asked quietly, "Who *is* that mug?"

"Weedon Scott," someone whispered. "He's a mining expert. I'd steer clear of him. He's all hunky with the officials."

"I thought he must be somebody," Keenan said. "That's why I kept my hands off of him at the start."

Chapter 13

WEEDON SCOTT

"It's hopeless," said Weedon Scott. "It's a wolf and there's no taming it."

"He's been tamed a'ready," Matt said. "D'ye see them harness marks across the chest? He was a sled dog at one time. And he was probably a good sled dog."

"But we've had him two weeks," Scott said, "and if anything, he's wilder than ever."

"Turn 'im loose for a spell," Matt said. "Could be the cage makin' 'im crazy."

"Won't he run away?" Scott asked.

Matt shrugged his shoulders. "Only way to find out is find out."

Matt grabbed a club and went over to the chained animal. The dog-musher unsnapped the chain and stepped back.

White Fang couldn't believe he was free. He saw the younger man toss him a piece of meat. He sprang away, and studied it from a safe distance.

"Major! No!" Matt shouted, but too late.

Major, the lead sled dog, had made a spring for the meat. At the instant his jaws closed on it, White Fang's closed on Major's throat. Matt's foot kicked at White Fang. White Fang tore a gash out of Matt's leg, then jumped back.

"He got me, all right," Matt said, holding his leg.

"I told you it was hopeless, Matt. There's only one thing to do," Scott said. He drew his revolver. "We can't have him attacking people."

"But I had no right to kick 'im, Mr. Scott," Matt argued. "Give the poor devil a chance. Please don't shoot 'im. I know he can be petted. Look at 'im. He knows he done wrong."

Scott put away the revolver. White Fang lowered himself down into the snow.

"You're sure?" Scott asked.

"Yes, I'm sure. He was petted at sometime in his life, wasn't he? He was a sled dog."

Scott believed the dog-musher, and slowly reached out his hand. "Here, good boy."

But the dog-musher was mistaken. As Weedon Scott approached, White Fang snarled.

Scott sat down several feet away. He remained quiet and made no movement. White Fang's snarl slowly became a low growl that grew softer and softer. Then Scott spoke. At the first sound of the man's voice, the hair rose on White Fang's neck. The growl rushed back up in his throat. But Scott made no movement and went on talking calmly.

After a long time, Scott held out a small piece of meat. White Fang pricked up his ears and looked at it suspiciously.

Scott tossed the meat on the snow at White Fang's feet. He smelled the meat carefully, but kept his eyes on Scott. Then he slowly ate the meat. Scott offered him another piece of meat. White Fang would not take it from the hand. Again Scott tossed it to him. Scott did this a few times. But one time, Scott held onto the meat.

Bit by bit, White Fang approached the hand. A low growl rumbled in his throat. He ate the meat, and nothing happened. Piece by piece, he ate all the meat, and nothing happened.

WHITE FANG

Scott went on talking. And then, Scott reached forth his hand. White Fang snarled and bristled and flattened his ears. But he didn't snap or spring away. The hand touched the ends of his bristling hair. White Fang shrank down under it. He could not forget all the evil that had been done against him at the hands of men.

The hand lifted and came down again in a kind, patting movement. Scott talked softly, and his hand patted gently.

"Well, I'll be gosh-swoggled!" exclaimed Matt, coming out of the cabin. White Fang leaped back, snarling savagely at Matt.

Weedon Scott stood and walked over to White Fang. He talked quietly to him, then slowly put out his hand and rested it on White Fang's head.

"You may be a number one, tip-top mining expert, all right," Matt said, "but you're a wild animal tamer, too! When you was a boy you shoulda run off to join a circus."

It was the beginning of the end for White Fang. It was the ending of the old life ruled by hate. It was the beginning of a new life—with Weedon Scott. It was Weedon Scott's patience and love that changed White Fang.

Weedon Scott was determined to tame White Fang. Each day he made it a point to pet him. White Fang grew to like this petting, but he never outgrew his growling. However, it was now a growl of contentment, and Scott knew this.

White Fang had never known such kindness, and his *like* for Weedon Scott grew to *love*. He felt protective of this man who treated him fairly and gently. He prowled about the cabin while the sled dogs slept. He listened for any stranger. The first night-visitor to the cabin fought him off with a club until Scott came to the rescue. Eventually, White Fang learned to tell the difference between friend and enemy. He let any man alone who stepped loudly to the cabin door. But he attacked any man who went softly and secretly.

White Fang was changing. He no longer roamed the woods, or hid at the corner of the cabin. Instead, he would wait for hours on the cabin steps for a sight of Weedon Scott's face.

In the late spring, Scott suddenly disappeared. White Fang had never seen a suitcase before, so he did not know what it meant. That night he waited in the cold on the front step for his master to return. But Scott never came.

In the morning, Matt opened the door and stepped outside. White Fang gazed at him sadly. The days came and went, but never Weedon Scott. White Fang, who had never known sickness, became so sick that Matt finally brought him inside the cabin. He wrote a letter to Scott:

"That wolf won't eat.
Mebbe he is going to die."

It was as Matt had said. White Fang lay on the floor of the cabin near the stove—without interest in food, in Matt, nor in life. Matt talked gently to him, but it made no difference. White Fang just turned his dull eyes upon the man, and then dropped his head back on his forepaws.

One night, Matt was startled by a low whine from White Fang. He had got upon his feet, his ears cocked toward the door. A moment later, Matt heard a footstep. The door opened, and Weedon Scott stepped in. The two men shook hands. Then Scott looked around the room.

"Where's the wolf?" he asked.

Then he discovered him, standing where he had been lying, near the stove. He had not rushed forward in the manner of other dogs. He stood, watching and waiting.

JACK LONDON

"Look at 'im wag his tail!" Matt exclaimed.

Weedon Scott strode halfway across the room toward him, at the same time calling him. White Fang came to him, not with a great bound, yet quickly. As he drew near, his eyes took on a strange expression.

"He never looked at me that way all the time you was gone," Matt commented.

Weedon Scott did not hear. He was squatting down on his heels, face to face with White Fang, petting him and listening to him growl. White Fang suddenly thrust his head forward and nudged his way in between the master's arm and body. And here, hidden from view except for his ears, no longer growling, he continued to nudge and snuggle.

One night, Scott and Matt sat playing a game of cards before going to bed. A wild scream of fear came from outside.

"The wolf's nailed somebody," Matt said.

"Bring a light!" Scott sprang outside.

Matt followed with the lamp, and by its light they saw a man lying on his back in the snow. His arms were folded across his face and throat. He was shielding himself from White Fang's teeth.

Weedon Scott grabbed White Fang and dragged him back. Matt helped the man to his feet. As he arose, Matt saw the beastly face of Beauty Smith. Matt let go quickly, as if he had touched fire.

At the same moment, Matt shone the lamp on two objects lying in the snow—a steel dog-chain and a stout club. Weedon Scott saw and nodded. Not a word was spoken. Matt laid his hand on Beauty Smith's shoulder and turned him around toward the woods. Beauty Smith scurried off.

Weedon Scott patted White Fang.

"Tried to steal you, eh? And you wouldn't have it! Well, well, he made a mistake, didn't he?"

They never saw Beauty Smith again.

Chapter 14

THE SOUTHLAND

"Listen to that, will you!" Matt exclaimed at supper one night.

Through the door came a low, anxious whine. Then came a long sniff, as White Fang smelled the air to make sure Scott was still inside.

"I do believe that wolf's on to you," said Matt.

"What the devil can I do with a wolf in California?" Scott demanded.

Silence followed. Again came the low, half-sobbing whine and the long, searching sniff.

"There's no denyin' he thinks a lot of you..." began Matt.

"I know what's best," snapped Scott.

339

Then came the day when, through the open cabin door, White Fang saw the suitcase on the floor. White Fang knew the meaning this time.

That night he lifted the long wolf-howl. He pointed his muzzle to the cold stars and told to them his woe. He knew that Scott was leaving and that he would be left behind.

The next day, two Indians arrived and carried away the luggage. After a while, Scott called White Fang into the cabin.

"I'm hitting the long trail, Wolf," he said gently as he patted him. "Now give me a growl—the last, good, good-bye growl."

But White Fang refused to growl. Instead, and after a sad, searching look, he snuggled in, burrowing his head out of sight between the master's arm and body.

"There she blows!" cried Matt as the steamboat on the Yukon River bellowed. "Get a move on!"

Scott and Matt hurried out the front door, leaving White Fang locked inside.

"You must take good care of him, Matt," Scott said. "Write and let me know how he gets along."

"Sure," the dog-musher answered. "But listen to that, will you!?"

White Fang was howling as dogs howl when their masters lie dead. The men turned and hurried toward the ship.

Onboard, Scott was shaking hands good-bye with Matt, who was preparing to go back ashore. But Matt's hand went limp as he stared at something behind Scott. Scott turned to see. Sitting on the deck of the ship several feet away was White Fang.

White Fang came to Scott when he called him. Fresh-made cuts lined White Fang's muzzle, and a gash oozed between his eyes.

"We plumb forgot the windows," Matt said. "He broke right through 'em!"

Scott was not listening. He was thinking quickly. The ship's whistle hooted. Men were scurrying down the gangplank to the shore. He looked at White Fang, then grasped Matt's hand.

"Good-bye, Matt. About the wolf—you needn't write. *I'll* write to *you* about him…

Matt understood and smiled.

As Matt went down the gangplank, Scott rubbed between White Fang's ears. "Now growl, Wolf," he said. "Growl."

White Fang did.

From the steamship, White Fang landed in San Francisco and boarded a train, where he was chained in a baggage car with his master's bags and luggage. When he came back out, San Francisco had gone. Before him was the smiling countryside, warm and sunny, lazy and quiet.

There was a carriage waiting, and a man and a woman approached. When the woman's arms wrapped around Scott's neck, White Fang became a raging demon!

Scott kept a tight hold on White Fang. "It's all right, Mother," Scott said. "Wolf thought you were trying to hurt me. He'll learn soon enough."

The bags were taken into the carriage, the man-animals followed, and White Fang ran along behind the carriage.

At the end of fifteen minutes, they reached the grounds of an estate. The carriage swung in through a stone gateway and on between a double row of arched walnut trees.

White Fang had little time to look around. Hardly had the carriage entered the grounds, when an angry collie ran toward him. White Fang was about to attack, until he realized the dog was a female. But the collie sprang.

"Here, Collie!" called the strange man sitting with Scott in the carriage.

Weedon Scott laughed, knowing White Fang would not attack a female dog. "Never mind, Father. The wolf will have to learn many things, and it's just as well that he begins now."

The carriage drove on, and still Collie blocked White Fang's way until he bumped her, knocking her over. The way made clear, he followed on with Collie yelping behind him.

As he rounded the house to the covered porch, White Fang came upon the stopped carriage. Almost immediately, he was knocked from his feet by a large deerhound. White Fang lunged to counterattack this new dog.

It was Collie that saved the hound's life. Just as White Fang was in the act of springing, Collie struck him, and again he was knocked off his feet.

The next moment Scott arrived. With one hand he held White Fang, while the father called off the other two dogs.

"I say, this is a pretty warm hello for a lone wolf from the Arctic," Scott said. "In all his life he's only been known once to go off his feet, and here he's been rolled twice in thirty seconds."

"Take Collie inside and leave the wolf and Dick to fight it out," suggested Scott's father. "After that they'll be friends."

"That might result in a funeral," laughed the master, knowing White Fang would show no mercy for another male.

"You mean that...?"

Weedon nodded his head. "I mean just that. I'm afraid Dick would be dead inside one minute—two minutes at the most."

He turned to White Fang. "Come on, you Wolf. It's you that'll have to come inside."

White Fang walked up the steps, keeping his eye on Dick. Once inside the house, he found no other dogs. Then he lay down at his master's feet, contented but on guard.

Chapter 15

THE SCOTT ESTATE

Here in Sierra Vista, which was the name of Judge Scott's place, White Fang quickly began to make himself at home. He had no further serious trouble with the dogs. The Scotts had allowed White Fang into the house, so Dick and the other dogs accepted him—and left him alone.

Not so with Collie. Though she accepted him, she continued to pick on him and nip at his legs. White Fang made it a point to keep out of her way. When he saw her, he got up and walked off.

White Fang learned to accept Weedon Scott's family, since they belonged to his master. There was Judge Scott, Weedon's father, and the Judge's

wife, Weedon's mother. There were the master's two sisters, Beth and Mary. There was Weedon Scott's wife, Alice, and his children, Weedon and Maud, toddlers of four and six. White Fang had disliked children ever since they mistreated him in the Indian village. When Scott's children first approached him, he snapped warningly. Scott gave him a sharp word, so White Fang let them pat him—though he didn't like it.

After a time, he grew fond of the family, and would lie on the porch at the Judge's feet as he read the paper. He allowed everyone to pat him. He even began to like the children.

This was a new life in a new land for White Fang. In the Northland, White Fang had hunted for food. He did not know that things were different here in the Santa Clara Valley of the Southland. Sauntering around the corner of the house in the early morning, he came upon a chicken that had escaped from the chicken yard. With a couple of leaps and a flash of teeth, he scooped up the frightened and squawking chicken. It was fat and tender. White Fang licked his chops.

Later in the day, he came upon another stray chicken near the stables. One of the stable hands ran to the rescue with a buggy whip. At the first cut of the whip, White Fang left the chicken to go for the man. The man cried out and staggered backward. He dropped the whip and shielded his throat with his arms. Suddenly, Collie appeared on the scene. Just as she had saved Dick the deerhound's life, she now saved the man's. She rushed upon White Fang as the man escaped into the stables, and White Fang backed away before Collie's wicked teeth.

"He'll learn to leave chickens alone," the master said that evening. "But I can't give him the lesson until I catch him in the act."

Two nights later came the act. After the chickens had gone to roost, White Fang climbed over the fence. A moment later he was inside the henhouse, and the slaughter began.

In the morning, the stableman laid out fifty dead white Leghorn hens for Weedon Scott to see. Angrily, Scott held White Fang's nose down to the hens. At the same time he cuffed him soundly. White Fang never raided a chicken roost again. He had learned the law.

But Judge Scott did not believe that the Wolf was cured. "Once a chicken-killer, always a chicken-killer," he said.

Weedon Scott did not agree with his father. "I'll tell you what I'll do," he challenged. "I'll lock Wolf in with the chickens all afternoon."

"But think of the chickens," said the Judge.

"*And* I'll pay you one dollar gold coin for every chicken he kills," Weedon went on. "But… if, at the end of the afternoon, Wolf has not harmed a chicken, you must solemnly repeat to him, 'Wolf, you are smarter than I thought.'"

The judge agreed to the test.

The whole family watched as White Fang was taken and left with the chickens. The "chicken-killer" simply lay down and went to sleep. Once he got up for a drink of water, but he calmly ignored the chickens. As far as he was concerned, they did not exist. He had learned the law.

He stayed all afternoon, then leaped the fence and sauntered back to the house. And on the porch, before the delighted family, Judge Scott sat face to face with White Fang. Slowly and solemnly, he repeated, "Wolf, you are smarter than I thought."

There was so much to learn. There were cats at the houses the master visited that must be let alone. And there were dogs everywhere that snarled at him and that he must not attack. And then, on the crowded sidewalks, there were persons aplenty. They would stop and look at him and, worst of all, pat him. Cats, dogs, turkeys, people—all these he must let alone. In fact, he began to think that he must leave all live things alone. And then, one day, he saw Dick scare up a jackrabbit and chase it. In the end, White Fang figured out that he must not touch any tame animal. But the other animals—the squirrels, and quail, and rabbits—were creatures of the Wild and were "fair game."

Chapter 16

THE CALL OF KIND

The months came and went. There was plenty of food and no work in the Southland, and White Fang lived fat and happy. Human kindness was like a sun shining upon him. He flourished like a flower planted in good soil.

And yet he remained somehow different from other dogs. The wolf and the Wild still lingered in him. He never chummed with the Southland dogs. He avoided his own kind and clung to the humans. The dogs feared him and greeted him with snarls, but they left him alone—except for Collie. She continued to annoy him whenever she found it possible.

Otherwise, all things went well for White Fang. Danger and hurt did not lurk everywhere about him. Life was soft and easy.

And he learned to romp and play with the master—to be tumbled down and rolled over. He did not even mind when Weedon would laugh at him. Long before, in his old life, laughter had made him frantic with rage. But he could not be angry with this master. As Weedon played and laughed, White Fang's jaws slightly parted, his lips moved a little, and a look of love and humor came into his eyes. He had learned to laugh.

The master went out on horseback a great deal. One of White Fang's chief duties was to go with him, but with no sleds or harness. He ran alongside, free and happy.

On one of these outings, a rabbit scampered in front of the horse. The horse was startled, and it reared up, throwing Weedon Scott. The master examined his injured leg and found it was broken. White Fang sprang in rage at the horse, thinking it had hurt his master.

"Home! Go home!" the master commanded.

White Fang did not want to desert the master. But again, Weedon commanded him to go home.

White Fang started to go—then returned and whined softly. The master talked to him gently, but seriously. White Fang cocked his ears.

"That's all right, old fellow, you just run along home," said Weedon. "Go on home and tell them what's happened to me," Scott said. "Home with you, you Wolf. Get along home!"

White Fang knew the meaning of "home." He turned and trotted away. Then he stopped and looked back over his shoulder. "Go home!" came the sharp command, and this time he obeyed.

The family was on the porch when White Fang arrived. He came up panting, covered with dust.

"Weedon's back," said Weedon's mother.

The children ran to meet White Fang, but he growled and tried to get past them.

"He makes me nervous around the children," said the children's mother.

"A wolf is a wolf," said Judge Scott. "There's no trusting one."

"But he is not *all* wolf," said young Beth.

"That's what Weedon says," replied the Judge. "But how does he know? Why, he looks—"

He did not finish. White Fang stood before him, growling fiercely.

"Go away! Lie down, sir!" Judge Scott commanded.

White Fang turned to Scott's wife. She screamed with fright as he seized her dress in his teeth and dragged on it till the fabric tore.

"I hope he is not going mad," said Weedon's mother. "I told Weedon that an Arctic animal—"

At this moment, White Fang did something the family had never heard him do before. He began to bark.

"He's trying to speak!" Beth announced.

"Something has happened to Weedon," his wife said earnestly.

They were all on their feet, now. White Fang ran down the steps, looking back for them to follow. He led them to his master, and they helped the injured man home. The "Wolf" had done what no wolf can do. He had barked and made himself understood.

After this event, he found a warmer place in the hearts of the Sierra Vista people. They admitted he was a wise dog—even though he was a wolf. Only Judge Scott refused to accept that White Fang had any dog qualities. To him, the animal was all wolf.

The days came and went. As the days grew shorter and White Fang's second winter in the Southland came on, he made a strange discovery. Collie became playful. He forgot that she had once annoyed him.

One day she led him off on a long chase though the pasture and into the woods. Side by side, White Fang ran with Collie—just as his mother, Kiche, and old One Eye had run long years before in the silent Northland forest.

—————— *Chapter 17* ——————

THE SLEEPING WOLF

It was about this time that the newspapers were full of the daring escape of a convict from San Quentin prison. He was a ferocious man. He had not been born right, and society had treated him poorly.

In San Quentin he fought the guards and other prisoners. The more fiercely he fought, the more harshly the guards handled him. This only made him fiercer. He was a beast—this Jim Hall.

During Jim Hall's third term in prison, he came up against a guard that was almost as great a beast as he. The guard treated him unfairly, lied about him to the warden, and tormented him.

365

One day Jim Hall killed this guard. He was sent to a small cell where he stayed for three years—completely alone. He never left. He saw no one. His food was shoved in to him. He growled like a wild animal. He hated all things.

And then, one night, he escaped. Three dead guards marked his trail through the prison to the outer walls. He was hunted day and night with bloodhounds. But Jim Hall had disappeared.

In the meantime, the Scott family nervously read the newspapers. The women were afraid, but Judge Scott laughed—though even he worried. For in his last days as a judge, Jim Hall had stood before him and was sentenced to *fifty years* in prison. And in the courtroom, Jim Hall had sworn that if he ever got free, he would come looking for the judge. Then Jim Hall went off to prison… and escaped.

White Fang knew nothing of all this. But he and Alice, the master's wife, shared a secret. Each night, after all of Sierra Vista had gone to bed, she arose and let in White Fang to sleep in the big hall. Now, the "wolf" was not a "house-dog," so early each morning she slipped down and let him out before the family was awake.

On one such night, while the house slept, White Fang awoke and lay quietly. A strange man had paused at the foot of the staircase. Up that staircase was the family White Fang knew to protect. The strange man's foot lifted.

White Fang gave no warning—and no snarl. Into the air he sprang and landed on the strange man's back, dragging him over backward.

There were revolver shots. A man's voice screamed in horror. Snarling followed, and a smashing and crashing of furniture and glass.

The house awoke in alarm. Weedon and Judge Scott came down the stairs. In the middle of smashed furniture, partly on his side, his face hidden by an arm, lay a man. Weedon turned the man's face upward. He was clearly dead.

"Jim Hall," said Judge Scott.

Then they turned to White Fang. He, too, was lying on his side. His eyes were closed, but the lids lifted to look at them, and the tail tried to wag. Then his eyelids dropped and went shut. His body relaxed and flattened out upon the floor.

"He's done for," muttered the master.

"We'll see about that," said the Judge, as he started for the telephone.

WHITE FANG

"Frankly, he has one chance in a thousand," announced the surgeon, after he had worked an hour and a half on White Fang. "One broken hind leg, three broken ribs, three bullet wounds, a great loss of blood... I should say he hasn't a chance in ten thousand."

"But he mustn't lose any chance," exclaimed Judge Scott. "Never mind the expense. Put him under X-ray—anything. Weedon, telegraph at once to San Francisco for Doctor Nichols. He must have the advantage of every chance."

White Fang received the best care available. The ladies nursed him. And White Fang won out on that one chance in ten thousand. For he had come from the Wild, where the weak do not survive. He clung to life with an iron will.

He lingered out the weeks in bandages and plaster casts, unable to move about. He slept long hours and dreamed much. Once again he lived in the den with Kiche. Or he crept to the knees of Gray Beaver. He ran from Lip-lip and the puppy pack. He lived again his days with Beauty Smith. At these times he whimpered and snarled in his sleep. The family looked on and said that his dreams were bad.

WHITE FANG

Then came the day when the last bandage and the last plaster cast were taken off. All Sierra Vista was gathered around. The master rubbed his ears, and the master's wife called him the Blessed Wolf. After several failed attempts, he stood on his four legs, tottering and swaying back and forth.

"The Blessed Wolf!" cheered the women.

"Yes. Blessed Wolf," agreed the Judge. "That will be the name for him."

"He'll have to learn to walk again," said the surgeon, "Take him outside."

Outside he went, like a king, with all the family around. He was very weak. He reached the lawn, rested, and then finally reached the stables. There in the doorway lay Collie with six pudgy puppies playing about her in the sun.

Collie snarled a warning, and White Fang was careful to keep his distance. The master helped one waddling puppy toward him, telling White Fang that all was well.

The puppy sprawled in front of him. White Fang cocked his ears and watched it curiously. Then their noses touched, and he felt the warm little tongue of the puppy on his jowl. White Fang's tongue went out and he licked the puppy's face.

WHITE FANG

The family clapped their hands and sent up cheers. White Fang was surprised, and looked at them in a puzzled way. The other puppies came sprawling toward him, to Collie's great disgust. He calmly permitted them to clamber and tumble over him as he lay with half-shut, patient eyes, drowsing in the sun.

THE END

WHITE FANG

JACK LONDON

John (Jack) Griffith London was born in 1876 and grew up in San Francisco. He left school at age fourteen and went on to hold many unusual jobs. He was an "oyster pirate," he worked for the Fish Patrol of San Francisco, and he worked on a seal-hunting ship that took him to Japan. He then traveled around the United States. In 1897, he joined the gold rush in the Klondike, in the far north of Alaska and Canada.

In his early twenties, Jack London knew he wanted to be a writer. He was a self-taught man who read and wrote constantly. He continued to travel, sail, and write—about the slums of London, the South Sea islands, boxing, life in the wilds, and life at sea. Some of his more famous works include *The Call of the Wild* (1903), *The Sea-Wolf* (1904), and *White Fang* (1906), which portray scenes and characters from his own experiences.

Jack London had a rich—sometimes wild—life. It was filled with adventure, but it was also filled with illness and private sadness. He died much too early at the age of forty in 1916.